DONNER UND BLITZKRIEG

BOOK ONE OF THE MINUTEMEN

Jeffrey Harlan

Confluent Press™

Library of Congress Control Number: 2024905030

ISBN: 979-8-9902609-0-0 (hardcover), 979-8-9902609-2-4 (paperback), 979-8-9902609-4-8 (ebook)

https://www.confluentpress.com
https://www.jeffreyharlan.com1

Thank you to my family and friends for your support and encouragement, especially to my wife, Megan, and the NOC Writing Community group on Discord.

PROLOGUE
Tuesday, May 1, 1945

Come quickly, son," Father said. It was dark; it must still be early in the morning. Father was dressed, as always, in his uniform: dark gray, immaculately clean, its high collar and martial tailoring announcing Father's importance to anyone who saw him. And Father was an important man, Erich knew. He was one of the advisers to the Führer himself.

Erich rose from his bed. He heard the distant thunder of artillery. It sounded louder this morning. He ran his hands through his close-cropped hair, which was the same shade of blond as his parents. He dressed in his Hitler Youth uniform, which was similar in cut to Father's own uniform, but black in color and with different insignia. Ever since the Soviets had begun their attack on Berlin, the older boys had been called upon to help defend the Fatherland as part of the *Volkssturm*—a citizen militia composed of older men and boys as young as thirteen—but Erich himself was still too young at ten years old. He wanted to do his part and join the older boys, and with the Soviet artillery shelling throughout the city, Erich thought he might still get his chance. It scared and excited him at the same time.

As Erich entered the dining room several minutes later, he saw his parents waiting for him at the table. "Come," Father said.

"Eat." Erich took his seat at the table as instructed, and began to eat his breakfast. It was warm and filling. Mother had always been a good cook; she took care to feed her family, as a proper Aryan woman should. Father and Mother both worked hard to fulfill their duties as Aryan parents, duties that Erich had learned extensively during his years in the Hitler Youth. Erich noticed that his parents were far quieter than usual this morning, and that they had woken him far earlier than usual. Something was clearly amiss, but he had no idea what that could be. The direct approach was necessary. "Father," he asked, "is something wrong?"

Father and Mother exchanged worried looks. Father returned his eyes to his plate. After a moment, he set down his fork and knife, then looked into Erich's eyes.

"*Der Führer* is dead," Father sighed in resignation. "So is Göbbels. The Soviet Army is about to completely overrun Berlin. Admiral Dönitz is now the new Führer... for however long the Reich will continue to exist." He sighed again, his head drooping. "We must leave. Today."

"Leave?" Erich asked. "Where will we go?"

"Argentina," Father replied. "The government there has been very... amenable to those wishing to leave Germany." As Erich cleared his plate, Father added, "Pack what you need, but we must travel light. We will leave as soon as you are ready, but don't expect to ever be able to return. Be sure to bring clothing that will not make us easily identifiable as Germans. We will change into that clothing once we are outside of the areas still controlled by the Reich."

—§—

As the sun began to rise, Erich and his parents made their way through the rubble of the ruined city center of Berlin.

"Herr General!" a voice called out from a guard station nearby. A Wehrmacht soldier came to attention and saluted. He was young, perhaps sixteen, and he looked uncertainly at Erich and Mother. Father noticed the soldier's gaze.

"I am taking my family to a safer location," Father said. "I have come for a vehicle to transport them."

"Nowhere is safe, Dieter," another voice came from behind Erich and his family. "You know this as well as I."

Father turned and smiled grimly. The guard saluted once again. It was one of Father's fellow generals, Viktor Hörst. Dressed in a uniform almost exactly like Father's, Hörst otherwise looked nothing like Father. He was short and barrel-chested, and his hair, only partially visible under his high-peaked uniform cap, was extremely dark. He wore round spectacles, but his eyes were nevertheless narrowed behind them. "Viktor," Father said. "I said safer, not safe. I am aware of the difference. This war is all but over. It is only a matter of time before Dönitz is forced to surrender. There is precious little that we can do at this point; keeping my family as safe as I can manage is the most important thing that I can now do."

"You would abandon the Fatherland?" Hörst asked. "Your duty—"

"I abandon nothing," Father replied. "As I said, and as you, too, are well aware, this war is finished. My command no longer exists; it was decimated by the Allies mere days ago. I must look to preserve my family, as there is nothing more that can be done to preserve the Fatherland."

"Where will you go?" Hörst asked.

"It is perhaps best that you not know," Father said, "but it is my hope that, in time, the Reich might be restored."

Hörst nodded, then addressed the guard. "Let them pass," he said. Turning back to Father, Hörst said, "Be safe, Dieter Eidelmann. I hope to see you again."

CHAPTER ONE
Thursday, December 18, 1952

Merry freakin' Christmas," Corporal Cliff Roberts said. He shivered and tried to zip his fiberglass-lined uniform parka higher, but it was already zipped as far as it would go. He adjusted his scarf so that it covered the lower half of his face, and his rubber "Mickey Mouse" cold weather boots, so nicknamed because of their bulky shape, squeaked as he walked on the frozen dirt. His M1 Garand rifle began to slip from his shoulder, and he grabbed the strap and hefted it back up against his ruck. Once the wooden stock of the rifle was back in place, he shoved his hands back into his pockets, his breath freezing into clouds as he muttered his intense disapproval of the Korean winter weather.

Private First Class Percival "Percy" van Norton, overhearing Corporal Roberts' muttered invective regarding the weather, struggled valiantly to contain his laughter. While Roberts hailed from the warmer climes of California, van Norton was a native of New York City, and thus well acquainted with cold winters. It was cold, to be sure, at a temperature very near freezing, but not so bitterly cold that van Norton felt the need to complain about it... yet.

The Korean War had been raging for more than two years, though none of the generals or politicians would call it a war; they used terms like "conflict" or "police action." Whatever they called it, people had been fighting and dying for years, and as far as van Norton was concerned, it was a war. Van Norton had been fighting in it for just over a year now, having been drafted in November 1951 at the age of eighteen, and he was more than ready for it to all be over so that he could go back home. He missed home: Christmas with his family, baseball games at Yankee Stadium, summers at the Hamptons, and spending an evening at the movies with his girl of the moment.

His thoughts were interrupted when a Willy's Jeep shot past him. He watched the vehicle bounce over the rough path that they laughingly called a "road," which his platoon was marching North on, toward communist-held territory. As it passed the front of van Norton's unit, there was a terrible explosion, and the jeep suddenly flipped into the air, dirt spewing from the ground that had been underneath it mere moments before. Time seemed to slow as van Norton watched in horror at the spectacle before him. The sergeant driving the jeep was thrown into the air, his helmet flying from his head and his arms pinwheeling at his sides, the angle at which he was ejected from the jeep's open passenger compartment sending him flying headfirst toward the ground. Meanwhile, the jeep spun twice in the air before slamming back down to earth. It rolled to a stop, pinning the now-unconscious sergeant beneath its shattered steel mass.

Adrenaline surged through van Norton's veins. As his brothers-in-arms took shelter, not knowing yet if the explosion was due to a land mine or enemy fire, van Norton ran toward the smoking hulk of the jeep. He started to pull at the bottom of the jeep, but before his mind could process what he was doing and tell him that there was no way that he could lift the vehicle by himself, he astonished himself by suddenly and effortlessly lifting the entire jeep above his head. Van Norton's mind raced. These jeeps weighed more than half a ton, yet it felt as though it weighed no more than a few pounds. He had always been strong, but never like this.

He stared in disbelief at the jeep above his head, then glanced down at the unconscious sergeant at his feet. He heaved the weight forward, intending to drop the metal hulk safely away from the wounded sergeant, only to watch in shock as it sailed far into the distance. He looked incomprehensibly at his hands. A shuffling noise to his side drew his attention, and he saw the other men in his platoon staring at him with looks ranging from astonishment to horror.

— § —

Lance Corporal Alexander Stevens shifted the M1 Garand rifle that he carried as he marched through the countryside of Korea. Drafted after he turned eighteen years old, he'd been with the First Marine Division for just over a year. Since March, his unit had been attached to the Eighth Army, and had been assigned as part of Operation Bootdrop. The strategy was designed to put more South Korean forces on the Main Line of Resistance, and other United Nations forces were reassigned. The First Marines found themselves on the far western end of the UN forces, defending a 35-mile stretch of land encompassing the Pyongyang-to-Seoul corridor. For months, the First Marines and their North Korean opposites had been trading the same outposts and scraps of land back and forth, and the fighting had been bitter and bloody.

Stevens scanned the horizon; while on patrol, the Marines had to be constantly vigilant, as North Korean forces could appear at any moment. This vigilance had saved his life and the lives of his fellow Marines on numerous occasions. This day was to be no exception. The hand signal to stop came up from another Marine, then fingers pointed to the northwest. Stevens brought his rifle to the ready, his eyes scanning the horizon. The report of a rifle came to Stevens' ears just as he spotted the form of a man, rifle raised in his general direction, then another, then several more. He crouched to a kneeling position, both to reduce the target that he presented to the enemy as well as to steady his own aim. He took aim at one of the North Korean soldiers in the distance, and returned fire.

After firing several rounds, most of which he was certain had found their targets, the all-too-familiar pinging sound of empty *en bloc* clips ejecting from the patrol's rifles began to fill the air. Stevens' own clip pinged out and away, and he quickly pulled out a fresh clip from his belt and reloaded. He took aim once again, and realized that more North Korean soldiers were emerging from behind the hill almost as quickly as his patrol could take them out. This continued for several minutes: Fire. Ping. Reload. Fire. Ping. Reload. The Marines had acquitted themselves well, but several had been wounded, and at least one was dead… and the North Korean forces were continuing to advance. Fire. Ping. Reload. Fire. Ping.

Stevens reached for his belt, and realized in horror that he was out of ammunition. "I'm out!" he called. He wasn't the first, apparently. The other Marines were quickly running low on ammunition as well. Even the M1917A1—a water-cooled Browning heavy machine gun—fell silent after another minute. And the North Koreans, though they had taken heavy losses, were continuing to advance.

"Fix bayonets!" his sergeant ordered. Stevens' stomach dropped. He pulled his bayonet from its sheath, and quickly snapped it into place at the end of the barrel of his rifle. Several Marines continued to fire, but the rate of fire had diminished significantly. The North Koreans raced toward their position, and Stevens steeled himself for close-quarters combat. A North Korean soldier charged, screaming, at Stevens, who held his ground against the terrifying onslaught. His eyes narrowed, and his grip on the wooden stock of his rifle tightened. Just as the enemy soldier closed the gap between them, Stevens adjusted his grip on the Garand and thrust the bayonet-tipped rifle forward. The blade plunged into the North Korean soldier's chest with a sickening, wet sound. The soldier's eyes widened in surprise and pain. He looked down at the bayonet, which was embedded to its hilt in his chest. He dropped his own weapon, and grabbed limply at the barrel of the Garand. He locked eyes briefly with Stevens, who pulled back on the rifle. The bayonet slipped out of the dying soldier, who slumped to the ground.

Stevens glanced quickly around, assessing the battle around him. The North Korean soldiers greatly outnumbered those of his own unit, which was quickly becoming overwhelmed. He lashed out with his bayonet again and again, felling enemy soldiers as quickly as he could manage. His training kicked into overdrive, and he meted out death efficiently and without mercy. After several minutes of fighting, the tip of his bayonet became lodged in one of the bones of its latest victim, and stuck fast. He tugged hard, but the blade barely budged. As he continued to pull in an effort to free his weapon, Stevens was tackled by another enemy soldier. They rolled away, the Garand and its bayonet staying gruesomely embedded in its last target. The North Korean soldier brought his own knife to bear, raising it to plunge into Stevens' body, but the Marine grabbed his enemy's wrist, fighting for his very life.

Holding the blade safely away from his own body, Stevens bashed his forehead against the skull of his enemy. The North Korean soldier lost his grip on the blade, which clattered to the ground mere inches from Stevens' head. Stevens threw his weight, rolling the pair until he was straddling his enemy. He drew back his fist, and punched the soldier in the jaw as hard as he could manage. The enemy soldier's body shuddered as the impact registered, and Stevens drew his fist back for another blow. He continued striking the man until he lost consciousness, then grabbed the knife and looked for another enemy within striking distance. He saw another North Korean soldier pummeling another Marine, but the pair was too far away to reach quickly. He flipped the knife in the air, grabbing it by the tip of the blade, then hurled it with all his strength. It sailed through the air, embedding itself deeply in the enemy soldier's back. The communist soldier threw his arms out and his head back in shock and pain, then toppled to the ground, one hand clutching desperately and futilely at the blade between his shoulders.

Stevens rose from his crouch, and ran toward another nearby foe. He clenched his fist, steeling himself for yet another mortal combat. Stevens felt the bundle of letters that he kept in one of the pockets of his uniform shirt bounce against his chest as he ran. The letters were mostly from his girlfriend, Evelyn, though a few were from his parents as well. He *had* to survive this. The thought of not getting home to see them again terrified him. All he had at this moment were his fists. It would have to be enough. He raised an arm as he neared the enemy soldier, who turned and looked at Stevens as he ran toward him.

Stevens swung at the soldier, who had inexplicably stopped and was staring at him, not bothering to defend himself at all. As the punch connected, Stevens realized why. His fist was glowing, surrounded by a crackling cloud of energy. The glow was so intense, he could even make out the faint shapes of the bones within his hand. The North Korean soldier dropped like a stone from the powerful impact of the blow. Stevens couldn't tell if he was unconscious or dead, and had neither time nor inclination to check. He glanced around, looking for his next target. He moved quickly, from one enemy soldier to the next, taking them down brutally and efficiently. The glow in his fist began to grow brighter, the cloud of energy expanding.

The North Korean soldiers began to run when they saw him coming. Stevens swung his fist at his latest target, but the soldier ducked away from the blow. He'd seen enough of his comrades felled in a single blow by that demonic fist, and didn't wish to join them so easily. Stevens swung again, his other fist now aglow as well. Again, he missed;

this foe was more wily than his compatriots. He thrust his hand out, this time to grab the man, but this time, when the North Korean soldier ducked away, a blast of energy issuing from Stevens' palm. The soldier fell to the ground, smoke rising from his scorched overcoat.

Stevens looked at his hands once again in shocked amazement. He had no idea how he was doing this, but he wasn't one to look a gift horse in the mouth: he was, himself, a weapon, and it was not something he was going to let go to waste when his fellow Marines were under assault and their supply of ammunition all but completely exhausted. Stevens stared down another North Korean soldier several yards away. He threw his open hand out once again, and as before, a burst of energy issued forth. It sped across the battlefield like lightning, and struck his target squarely in the chest. The soldier was launched backward into the air, and landed hard on his back. Stevens quickly began to fire blasts of energy across the battlefield at the enemy.

It didn't take long for the North Korean soldiers to realize that Stevens had become the biggest threat on the battlefield, and they began to disengage from fighting with the other Marines. They began to swarm around and encircle Stevens, who continued to fire blast after blast at the approaching mob. The number was simply overwhelming, however, and the circle around him tightened moment by moment. First one soldier, then another, piled on Stevens' back. In moments, he found himself at the bottom of a pile of men. They punched, kicked, and stabbed at him with their knives. One of the knives dug into his thigh, and the pain was excruciating. Stevens pushed back, trying to stand, trying to get this mass of humanity off of him. His entire body began to glow. He roared, and as he made his way to his feet, he released a wave of energy. North Korean soldiers flew in all directions, thrown from Stevens by this incredible, inexplicable power he suddenly possessed. Gravity returned them to the ground with unyielding force, and they lay, smoking and unmoving, either unconscious or dead. Stevens rose unsteadily to his feet, the glow emanating from his body beginning to fade. His ragged breathing sounded almost like the panting of an exhausted dog, and he struggled to slow his inhalations to a more natural pace. He tried to step forward, but staggered from the knife wound in his leg. He stumbled, and fell to his knee, his fists stopping him from collapsing completely.

"Medic!" someone called. One of the other Marines rushed to Stevens' side. "Get the medic over here!" he yelled. The Marine put a reassuring hand on Stevens' shoulder. "You're gonna be all right, Lance Corporal. We're all gonna be okay."

CHAPTER TWO
Monday, January 5, 1953

Percy van Norton shifted his weight from his left to his right foot as he stood in the at ease position, his hands clasped behind his back. After the incident with the jeep, he had been ordered to report to Fort Leonard Wood, Missouri. The place had been nicknamed "Fort Lost in the Woods," and for good reason: it was almost literally in the middle of nowhere, several hours' drive from the nearest major cities, and was surrounded by forests in the foothills of the Ozark Mountains. It was the home of an Army basic training facility, though not the one that van Norton had processed through back in 1951.

Van Norton looked around. The others weren't just in the Army like him, but wore uniforms from multiple branches. There were about a dozen others here, representing the Army, Air Force, Navy, and Marine Corps. One person even wore a uniform that he couldn't quite place. It looked similar to that worn by the Navy sailors, but not quite. Coast Guard? What was going on? Why were all of these people here?

"At-ten-SHUN!" a voice rang out. Van Norton and everyone else in the room snapped to attention. "Officer on deck!" One of the sailors, apparently.

"At ease," the officer in question ordered. Van Norton and the others returned to the at ease position. "I'm Captain Don Wright, U.S. Army. I'm sure you're all wondering what the hell you're doing in Missouri, instead of back in Korea." There were nods and murmurs of assent. "All of you have demonstrated... remarkable abilities." Van Norton and the others all began to look at one another in surprise. He wasn't the only one? "Each of you has demonstrated a unique combat effectiveness with those abilities. Uncle Sam has brought all of you together, because we hope that we can put those abilities to better use.

"You're going to be a team. A new, joint forces, special operations unit, composed entirely of soldiers, sailors, airmen, and Marines with... well, for lack of a better word, super powers."

"Like the Justice Society?" someone asked.

"Not quite," Captain Wright said. "You won't be wearing capes or tights. You're still in the United States military, and you'll be using your talents to fight for your country. It's more like Captain America. A whole unit of Captain Americas. But you need to learn how to use your abilities effectively, and how to use them together. You're going to be training here at Fort Leonard Wood, until we think you're ready to go back out to Korea and help us win the war. For now, get to know each other. We'll reconvene for a briefing at thirteen-hundred hours. As you were." Wright turned and left the room.

Van Norton turned to the dark-haired Marine standing near him. No name tag; Marines didn't wear them. He did see a rank patch that looked just like his own. He extended his hand. "Private First Class Percy van Norton," he introduced himself. "Private...?"

"Lance Corporal," the Marine corrected. "Alex Stevens." He took van Norton's proffered hand and shook it, then winced. "That's a hell of a grip you've got, van Norton."

Van Norton was confused. "You mean you're not strong, too?"

"No more than any other guy," Stevens said. "I can shoot energy from my hands."

"I thought we all had the same thing going for us," van Norton said.

"Apparently not," Stevens agreed. "Maybe we should take an inventory or something." He turned to a nearby sailor. "Hey, squid," he said. "What's your thing?"

"My thing?" the sailor asked. His complexion was darker, and his hair nearly jet black. He reminded van Norton of the Puerto Ricans he'd seen back in New York.

"Yeah," Stevens said. "This guy's got superstrength, and I can shoot energy from my hands."

"Oh," the sailor said. "I can... this is gonna sound crazy, but... I can turn my body into anything I touch."

"Crazier than shooting energy outta my hands?" Stevens asked.

"Good point," the sailor replied.

"So," van Norton asked, "if you touch a tire iron—"

"I can make my body turn into metal," the sailor finished.

"Damn," van Norton muttered. Several of the others began to gather around them, and before long, everyone had shared their unique abilities with the others. Someone said he could fly. Another could breathe underwater. Despite Captain Wright's assertion to the contrary, van Norton was sure of one thing: comic books really were becoming a reality. How long would it be before some damned fool decided to try becoming an honest-to-God superhero?

— § —

Tuesday, January 20, 1953

Van Norton strained and lifted the platform above his head. The veins in his neck bulged and his jaw was clenched. His teeth ground together, and his eyes were closed. All around him, cheers and chanting urged van Norton on. He held the platform aloft for nearly a full minute, then slowly lowered it to his shoulders and crouched until he felt the contact as the bottom of the platform settled atop the risers mounted in the floor.

Van Norton stood, stepping away and turning back to the platform. Atop it were several stacks of weights, both from barbell sets and improvised; they had switched to the platform after the first day of training, when the bar snapped in half under all of the weight placed upon it. That weight wasn't even enough to make van Norton breathe hard, let alone sweat, though it had earned him a nickname that he feared would never go away: Strongman. He had held the barbell, which was laden with so much weight that it bent—before it snapped in half— above his head in a single hand like a circus strongman. The name caught on instantly.

Another man stepped up to the platform. Chuck Hardy was a sailor with powers virtually identical to van Norton's, and like him, he had also already earned himself a nickname. Hardy was a large black man, and hadn't had a chance to get a haircut in quite some time when his powers appeared and he was transferred to Fort Leonard Wood. Although technically still within regulation length, his hair had been on the extreme end of what was allowed under the Navy's dress and appearance regulations. He had finally had the opportunity to get a haircut a few days after arriving at the Army post which, somewhat inevitably, led to good-natured, joking references to the biblical story of Samson, who lost his strength when his hair was cut. Van Norton had furthered the joke by "challenging" Hardy to a contest, where they would lift this insanely heavy platform of weights.

The "contest" had been delayed several times, thanks to delays in obtaining the equipment needed to create the platform after their original weight sets were destroyed. It had been nearly two weeks, and this was the first opportunity anyone had had to use the new platform. Delays like these had become typical for the new unit, as they were inventing new testing and training methods as they went, and trying to do so in secret, as their very existence was still classified.

Hardy stepped up and crouched under the platform, just as van Norton had before him, and the rest of the soldiers, sailors, airmen, and Marines assigned to the unit cheered him on with a chant of "Samson! Samson!" which they repeated over and over again. Hardy planted his feet and set his back and shoulders against the platform. He gripped the handles welded into place on the bottom of the platform's surface. With a grunt, he pushed, lifting the platform as he stood. He roared, yelling in both exertion and triumph as he lifted the platform above his head, and everyone began to cheer.

— $ —

Wednesday, January 28, 1953

Alex Stevens shivered slightly as the doctor placed what looked like small suction cups with wires attached to them to points across his chest, neck, arms, and head, then secured them in place with small pieces of fabric medical tape. Doctor Ezekiel Gillespie was new, and had been brought in to analyze everyone's powers. He had arrived over the weekend, and had spent the last several days doing these tests on every member of the unit. Once again, their training had been brought to a screeching halt.

"So," Doctor Gillespie asked as he taped down a sensor lead to Stevens' head, "they call you Nucleus?"

"Better than Nuclear Man," Stevens replied. "Thank God *that* one didn't stick."

"Hmm," Gillespie murmured. Stevens' eyebrows furrowed.

"What?" Stevens asked. Gillespie cleaned up the supplies from beside Stevens on the raised examination table.

"Well," Gillespie replied, "your powers *aren't* nuclear." Stevens' eyes widened in surprise. Before he could speak, however, the doctor continued, "I checked you with a Geiger counter earlier; the needle didn't budge. These sensors will give me a better understanding of what's actually going on, but at a guess, I'd have to say you're creating a plasma of some kind."

"A what?" Stevens asked.

"A plasma," Gillespie repeated. "It's another state of matter: solid, liquid, gas, and plasma. Think of it as a very energized form of gas."

"How?" Stevens asked after a moment.

"How are you doing that?" the doctor asked, clarifying the question. Stevens nodded. "Well, that's the million-dollar question, isn't it? That's what I'm hoping these tests will tell us." He checked his instruments, flipped a few switches, and the ticker-tape printers began slowly churning out numbers and squiggly lines. "Go ahead and turn on your power for me." Stevens lifted his right hand, which began to glow. The air crackled from the energy, and the glow from his hand intensified until the outline of the bones in his hand were visible. The doctor's instruments began spewing out streams of paper.

"Excellent," Doctor Gillespie said, studying the data. "It looks like your body is producing intense levels of energy, which is turning the molecules in the air around you into the plasma that you produce. I bet there'll also be some X-Rays being produced, which might be why we can see through your skin now." He checked his data again, gave another "Hmm," and continued thinking aloud. "Then again, that could also be caused by something else. I'm not reading significant levels of X-Rays. No gamma rays, either. Very interesting. Very little change in temperature, too. It seems to be a cold plasma."

"Cold?" Stevens asked. "It doesn't feel cold."

"Cold is relative," Gillespie replied. "Most plasmas are thousands of degrees. Yours is barely above room temperature." He looked Stevens over with an appraising eye, inspecting the young Marine from head to toe. "Can you generate the plasma from anywhere else on your body, or is it localized to your hands?"

"No," Stevens replied. Then, after a moment's thought, he amended, "Maybe. I haven't tried." He thought some more, and the doctor watched, waiting patiently as the instruments continued to spit out reams of ticker tape data. "Actually," Stevens said, "I think I have. When I first used my.. my *powers, I think I made it explode from my whole body.*" *The doctor nodded, thoughtfully.*

"It's possible, then," Gillespie began, "that you could fly." Stevens' jaw dropped in speechless silence. The doctor smiled, and continued, "Given enough thrust—projected from your feet, perhaps—you could launch yourself into the air like a rocket." Stevens stared at the doctor. His entire world had just changed once again.

— § —

Wednesday, March 25, 1953

After nearly two months of testing, Doctor Gillespie and the other doctors left, and training had finally resumed. It was a mess.

The members of the team had been drawn from every military branch, and their training to date had been very different, due to the needs of each branch. The Marines had excelled at individual and squad-level combat, and their Army counterparts were not far behind, but the Navy and Coast Guard sailors and the Air Force airmen had far less training in that kind of combat. They excelled, instead, at looking at the bigger picture of the fight, as the focus of their training had been in more technical and strategic areas. They all lacked experience and skill in the use of their powers, particularly when under the stresses of combat. The soldiers and Marines were more easily able to overcome this, but they also needed a great deal of training.

A dramatic example of this had just occurred the day before. Senior Airman Jack Knapp, a dark-haired man who could turn his body into a mass of blue fire, had taken flight during a training exercise in one of the many wooded areas of the base. Knapp, who had been nicknamed the Blue Flame by his teammates for obvious reasons, was attempting to lay down a wall of fire to stop the aggressor force from advancing when things went sideways.

The lead man in the aggressor force, a blond Coast Guard sailor named Lewis Binder, had the ability to run at super-speed, and had been nicknamed the Silver Streak by the others. When Blue Flame unleashed his fire wall, Silver Streak attempted to outrun it at super-speed. Blue Flame then attempted to create a flaming loop around Silver Streak.

Within seconds, the woods were engulfed in fire. A flaming tree split in half, and would have crushed Army Corporal Fred Larkin, nicknamed Lightning because he'd discovered his electrical-based powers after being struck by a bolt of lightning while on patrol in Korea. At the last instant, Army Sergeant Joe Higgins dove to protect Lightning with his own invulnerable body, earning himself the nickname of the Shield in the process.

The fire burned for several minutes before Blue Flame and Senior Airman Ray O'Reilly, who had been nicknamed Firebrand, managed to extinguish the conflagration with their powers. The blaze had attracted quite a lot of attention, however, and the team's existence soon became known to the public: the incident had happened too near the edge of the base, and a civilian boy who had been bird-watching in the area had managed to take pictures, which circulated nationwide in less than a day.

The team's leadership couldn't do much about the photos or the press frenzy that followed. Instead, while the military's public affairs units did what damage control they could, the team's leadership focused on what they *could* do: the team was taken back to what amounted to remedial basic training. The first month was dedicated to each member gaining fine control over their powers. From there, the focus shifted to using those powers as a team: tactics and strategies, which powers could be combined for greater effect, and which combinations should be avoided. Finally, nearly seven months after everyone had been brought together, the team was ready to be sent out for a real mission.

Then the other shoe dropped.

— § —

Monday, July 27, 1953

"A cease fire?" Air Force Sergeant Enrique Alvarez asked.

"That's correct," Captain Wright said, addressing the unit. After the facts of the existence of superhumans and of the unit itself had leaked and become public knowledge, the press had finally settled on a name for the unit: Team Liberty. Pressure for them to make their entrance into the war had mounted as the weeks had turned into months. And now, when they were finally at a point when everyone felt that Team Liberty was ready for action… there was no more action to be had.

"We will not be deploying back to Korea," Wright continued. "The terms of the cease fire specify that both sides are to ensure a complete cessation of hostilities, and bringing additional forces from the U.S. to South Korea—particularly superhuman forces—would only serve to escalate the tensions that the diplomatic corps is trying to reduce. Until we hear otherwise, we stay put."

"Sir," one of the soldiers—Private Isaac Jameson, who could fly—interjected, "most of us here are draftees. Won't we be going back home soon?"

"The conflict isn't quite over yet, private," Wright answered. "Rest assured, the terms of your enlistments will be honored. I don't doubt that many of you will be going back to your homes before too long."

Chapter Three

Wednesday, November 18, 1953

Alex Stevens packed his belongings into his duffel bag. The war was over, and now, too, was his enlistment in the United States Army. It was time for him to go back home to Brooklyn. Likewise, his new friend, Percy van Norton, would be going back home to the Bronx. They had both been drafted in 1951 at the age of eighteen for two-year terms.

He fastened the clasp at the top of the bag, sealing all of his possessions within. He threw the bag over his shoulder, and paused at the doorway of his barracks, looking back at what had been his home for much of the past year.

A few of the others from Team Liberty were still inside. Fully half the team had completed the terms of their enlistments over the past few months since the end of the war and they had gone home. Stevens and van Norton were the last of those who would be leaving, while Chuck "Samson" Hardy, Jason "Mimic" Ochoa, Tom "Typhoon" Sanders, Ray "Firebrand" O'Reilly and Fred "Lightning" Larkin were staying. Some still had another year left on their enlistments, and a few had opted to reenlist.

Stevens turned and walked outside, where he found van Norton waiting, his own duffel bag on the ground at his feet. Stevens and van Norton, coincidentally, had both been drafted at about the same time, and would be traveling back to New York together. The air was cool, and the leaves had turned and were falling in pools on the ground around the trees. It would soon be Thanksgiving, and Stevens was very thankful to be going home safely. His wounds from the war had healed, and now he had the rest of his life to look forward to.

One of the post shuttle buses pulled up, and Stevens and van Norton stepped aboard. They rode in companionable silence as the bus took them toward the main gate, where a taxi would be waiting to take them to the nearest train station. From there, they would ride the rails back to New York City, where their families would be waiting for them. Where Evelyn would be waiting for Stevens.

He hadn't seen her in two years, though they had kept in contact through the mail; he'd saved all of her letters, and reading them had helped buoy his spirits when the fighting in Korea had seemed bleakest. He hadn't been allowed to reveal to anyone that he was a member of Team Liberty; though the public had discovered that the team existed, the identities and exact abilities of its members still remained classified as a national secret. Stevens didn't know how he would tell his family—or Evelyn—about his abilities. He wasn't part of Team Liberty anymore, so he figured that it didn't matter if he told them about his abilities. He wouldn't explicitly say that he had been in the unit, but if they made that deductive leap on their own, he doubted that he'd get into any kind of trouble over it.

Over the past eleven months, he'd learned so much about his abilities... his *powers*. The scientists assigned to work with Team Liberty still didn't know exactly how they worked, but they'd confirmed that his body was able to generate plasma, instead of the original assumption that his powers were somehow nuclear-based. Despite this, the original nickname of "Nucleus," like so many in military life, stuck. At least it sounded better than van Norton's nickname; he'd been saddled with being called "Strongman." Fighting a nickname in the military was always doomed to failure, so they had accepted and eventually embraced the nicknames, even if they harbored some friendly jealousy for their teammates who had gained far better-sounding nicknames. Even Captain Wright—who could fly and had some super-strength, it turned out—got one. Captain America was taken, so he was dubbed Captain Freedom.

The pair exited the bus after it came to a stop at the main gate, far from the enlisted barracks where they had boarded. The base was so large that it had taken them nearly forty-five minutes to cross, thanks largely to the bus making multiple stops at the post exchange, commissary, movie theater, chow halls, and numerous other points in between throughout the enlisted barracks, family housing, officers' quarters, and unit headquarters offices. Military bases were designed to be small communities that could be largely self-sufficient if the need ever arose for the gates to be closed; though resupply would have to be made for food, fuel, and other necessities, the bases could remain sealed off for significant stretches of time, until whatever threat that necessitated such drastic action had—hopefully—passed.

Stevens and van Norton walked to the visitor parking lot near the guard shack at the main gate. Their taxi was already there, waiting for them. The driver was an older man, with graying hair and an expanding midsection. He had a salt-and-pepper beard that was closely trimmed, and wore a flat cap to cover the early stages of male pattern baldness. He rolled down the window, looked out, and asked, "You two headed for the train station?"

"Yes, sir," Stevens said. The taxi driver opened his door and stepped out. He opened the trunk of the car, and tossed the duffel bags into it before closing it. He opened the back door so that Stevens and van Norton could get into the cab, and shut it behind them once they were inside. He got back into the driver's seat, put the car in gear, and began to pull away from the visitor's parking lot.

"You boys back from Korea?" the taxi driver asked, placing an emphasis on the first syllable of the country's name. Stevens noticed the man's taxi license, prominently displayed on the dashboard. Next to the driver's photo, his name was printed in clear, blocky letters: Gregory Dewey.

"Yes, sir," van Norton said. Neither of them was about to confess to a complete stranger the circumstances surrounding their return from Korea, and it wasn't a total lie, after all. "Our tour is up, and we're mustering out. Going back home."

Dewey nodded. Clearly, he had provided transportation for many soldiers who had processed through Fort Leonard Wood at the end of their enlistments. "Where you boys heading? Where's home?"

"The Bronx," van Norton said.

"Brooklyn," Stevens added.

"Brooklyn!" Dewey exclaimed. "You a Dodgers fan? Ooo-wee, that was a heck of a series! A hundred and five wins!"

"I used to go watch the games at Ebbets Field, before I was drafted," Stevens said. "I guess I'll be able to again when the next season starts up."

Dewey continued an amiable conversation with Stevens and van Norton for the rest of the drive to the train station, which took quite some time, given how far Fort Leonard Wood was from St. Louis, and they made sure to tip him well. More than two hours after picking Stevens and van Norton up at the Army post, Dewey opened the door for them once again, and handed off their duffel bags as he pulled them from the trunk. He wished them well, and they bade him farewell, then Stevens and van Norton turned and walked into the train station.

Once inside, they went to the will-call ticket window. An attractive young woman with bright red hair was behind the window, and she smiled broadly at the pair as they approached the window.

"How can I help you, boys?" she asked.

"We're here to pick up our tickets to New York," Stevens said. "Names are Stevens and van Norton."

The young woman pulled out an expanding file folder, and flipped through the tabs. She rifled through several pieces of paper within, then pulled out a number of tickets, bundled into two stacks, each bound by a large paper clip. She slid the bundles under the window, and continued to smile at them. "Here you go, boys," she said. "Have a good trip!"

Stevens grabbed the bundles. He checked the names printed on them, then handed one stack to van Norton. They smiled back at the young woman, then turned and began to walk toward the loading platforms. It was nearly noon, and there was almost an hour until their train was scheduled to depart, so they made a detour to a small diner attached to the train station. After they had taken in a leisurely lunch, the pair boarded their train, and began the two-day trip to New York City.

— $ —

Friday, November 20, 1953

Stepping into Grand Central Station, Stevens and van Norton were both ambushed by their families. They were embraced by their parents, Stevens' sister, and several assorted relatives who had made the trip to greet them upon their arrival back in New York City. Though neither family had met before, they had apparently shared stories of their boys while waiting for them to arrive, and handshakes and hugs were shared all around. Everyone was excited and relieved to see their boys safely home from the war.

The excited reunion lasted for several minutes, but eventually all decided that it was time for the families to return to their homes. Stevens and van Norton bade one another farewell, but vowed to keep in contact. The friendship that they had formed over the past year at Fort Leonard Wood was not something they wished to ignore. Their opposition over baseball aside—where Stevens was a lifelong Dodgers fan, van Norton was equally enamored of the Yankees—the pair had discovered that they had a great deal in common. They arranged to meet in two days, to give themselves time to reunite with their families. They went their separate ways: Stevens and his family caught the subway to Brooklyn, while van Norton and his family had a car waiting to take them to the Bronx.

— $ —

Saturday, November 21, 1953

Stevens woke with a start. Glancing around, he quickly realized that he was in his old bedroom at his parents' home in Brooklyn. It had just been a nightmare. A memory, really, of one of the many battles he'd fought in during the war. He'd seen so many of his friends die over the past two years, and Stevens feared that he was doomed to repeat the experience for the rest of his life. At least he didn't have those nightmares every night, and they seemed to be happening less frequently.

Sitting up on the edge of the mattress, Stevens rubbed his eyes with the palms of his hands, and wiped the sleep from their corners as his fingertips passed over them. After a moment, he collected himself, then stood. He was slightly unsteady on his feet; the knife wound to his right thigh, though long since healed, still gave him a twinge of discomfort from time to time. Nearly two years in Korea, and it wasn't until his final battle that he was wounded. It could have been worse, he reminded himself.

He dressed, but civilian clothing felt odd after so long wearing uniforms. He gazed at his uniform, which hung in his closet, for several moments before closing the closet and stepping into the hallway. He walked over to the dining room, where he could already smell bacon and eggs on the stove. He sat at the table next to his father, who was reading his newspaper, just as he did every morning. Stevens looked very much like a younger version of his father; they were both slender, dark-haired men with fair complexions, though his father was adding more gray hair and lines on his face as the years passed.

"Good morning, Alex," his father said. "Did you sleep all right?" That was not a subject he wanted to discuss with his father.

"Fine," he lied. He grabbed a piece of toast and began to butter it.

"Son," his father said, lowering his paper and looking Stevens in the eyes. "You know that I fought in the Pacific in the last war. I know what it was like coming home after that. If you ever want to talk about it, you can talk to me, or I can introduce you to some people at the VFW. You don't have to keep it bottled up."

"Thanks, dad," Stevens said, "but I'm fine. Honest." He took a bite out of his toast and chewed. "What I need is to find a job and a place to live." He reached over and took the classified section of the newspaper, which was folded on the table next to his father. "Maybe there's something in the classifieds."

His father gently grabbed his wrist. He tensed, his reflexes from years of combat readying him to fight, but he willed himself to relax. His father clearly noticed the subtle change, but aside from releasing his grasp on Stevens' wrist and arching an eyebrow, he said nothing of it. "You haven't even been home a day, son," he said instead. "Give yourself some time to readjust to civilian life. You're welcome to stay here with us for a while."

Stevens sat back in his chair, nodding. He read the headlines on his father's newspaper. It seemed like it was nothing but doom and gloom: Celebrations of the anniversary of the communist revolution, China's role in the expansion of communism, unrest in Italy and Israel, fighting in French Indochina. Closer to home, the news seemed little better:

robberies, corruption trials, murders. There had to be better news in the world.

He finished his breakfast and cleared his place at the table. Taking his dishes to the kitchen, his mother stepped into his path. Lightly chiding him, she took his dishes and walked over to the sink. Stevens grabbed his coat. He told his parents that he was going out for a walk, and left their home. He made his way down the stairwell of the building and out into the chilly November morning, exchanging greetings with neighbors who recognized him, and who all expressed their happiness in seeing him home safely.

After walking for several blocks, Stevens stopped in front of another tall brownstone. He paused, and stood in front of the building for some time, unsure of how to proceed. A lot had happened over the last two years.

"Are you gonna come in, or what?" a playful woman's voice asked. Stevens looked up and saw Evelyn standing at the doorway of the brownstone. She was twenty years old, and had dated Stevens since the pair met in high school, six years earlier. She had long, dark hair, and the bright red lipstick she wore made her broad smile visible from across the street. She wore a knee-length blue dress with a white floral print, drawn tightly around her waist with a belt made of the same fabric.

Stevens climbed the steps of the brownstone and embraced Evelyn. They held each other tightly and in silence for nearly a full minute, then Evelyn led him inside and up the steps to her family's home. Once inside, he removed his coat, and was greeted by Evelyn's parents. Her father smiled broadly and gave him a firm handshake and a clap on the shoulder, while her mother, crying happily, embraced him tightly. He returned their welcome with a smile of his own, and made friendly conversation for several minutes before they left the room, leaving him alone with Evelyn.

"I missed you," she said.

"I missed you, too," he replied. After a brief silence, he continued, "Your letters helped me get through some hard times. Thank you for writing them."

"Of course," she said. After a few more moments of silence, she added, "I'm sorry I couldn't meet you at the station yesterday."

"It's all right," Stevens said. "I understand. It was the middle of the day on a Friday. There were plenty of people there, between my family and van Norton's."

"Van Norton?" Evelyn asked.

"A soldier I met," Stevens explained, "at Fort Leonard Wood, after I came back from Korea; he's from the Bronx. We both got out of the military at the same time, and came home on the same train." Fortunately, Evelyn didn't know enough about how the military worked to ask why a Marine was processing through an Army post, and Stevens wasn't ready to explain what he'd been doing for the last four months after the war ended. "He's a good enough guy, for a Yankees fan."

— § —

Percy van Norton's eyes fluttered open. He sat up quickly in bed, momentarily disoriented. The disorientation passed quickly, however, and he realized that he was in his bed at his home in the Bronx. He pushed aside the luxurious, silky sheets and thick, downy comforter, and swung his legs over the edge of the bed. He sat there quietly for a moment, gathering his thoughts.

Van Norton stood next to his large, comfortable bed. His pajamas began to cool against his skin, the warmth they'd accumulated from his body heat during the night drawn away by the chilly November air. He walked across the room, his bare feet chilled by the cool carpet, and stoked the pile of wood in the fireplace. The wood shifted at the touch of the iron poker, but generated no sparks or warmth; the fire had long since died out while he slept. Van Norton returned to his bed, where he stepped into his plush slippers, then made his way over to his closet. He pulled out a thick robe, which he threw around himself as he searched through his wardrobe, deciding on what clothes he should wear for his first day back in his civilian life.

After he made his selection, he set his clothes on the end of his bed. He stepped into the hallway, and his slippered feet made a soft padding sound as he walked to the bathroom. He turned on the shower and waited as the water warmed up. Van Norton stared at his reflection in the mirror as steam began to build. He felt odd, like he barely recognized the man who stared back at him from the glass. He continued to examine the near-stranger until the mirror became opaque from the steam that had built up in the bathroom. Reluctantly, he turned away, drew back the shower curtain, and stepped into the stream of hot water that issued forth from the shower head.

Van Norton began to lather up with the bar of soap, and paused as his hands crossed the network of scars that had built up on his body during his time in Korea. He realized that they were barely visible, nowhere near what they had been just a few weeks ago. If this kept up, he thought, his skin might even be as unmarred as it had been before he had been drafted.

Until two years ago, van Norton had never had to truly work for anything in his life. His family came from old money, and their estate was enormous. He had attended private schools, had tutors, and had been handed virtually anything he had desired. When he had been drafted, he could easily have found a way out of it, with his family's connections, but something inside him had resisted that idea. His parents had raised him to appreciate the privilege that the family enjoyed, and had impressed upon him that he had a responsibility to use his wealth and power to help those less fortunate. His father was a physician, and helped others as a healer. His grandfather had been a powerful business magnate, and employed thousands of people in his businesses. When he was called upon to serve his country during a time of war, could he then do anything else?

War had changed him. His wealth and privilege meant nothing in the military. There, he was a lowly private, just like any other young man. He advanced through his own capabilities, and endured the same hardships as everyone else. For the first time in his life, he came to realize just how spoiled he had been, just how much had been simply handed to him, and how much he truly didn't know about the world around him. He had made a few friends, but unlike many of them, he made it back home.

Speaking of friends, van Norton thought, *I wonder how Stevens is adjusting*. He turned off the water and drew back the shower curtain. He stepped out of the shower, his feet cushioned by a thick, carpeted shower mat. He grabbed a large, fluffy towel and began to dry himself off. Van Norton wiped the fog of condensation from the mirror as he continued to towel off. He paused once more, and stared at his reflection in the mirror.

Though still looking almost like a stranger to his eyes, his reflection seemed a little less unfamiliar. He knew that he couldn't just step back into his old life. The last two years had changed him too much. Something needed to change, but he didn't know what that was.

— § —

Stevens walked into the store on the corner near his family's home; the store was owned by an Italian man named Vincent Giordano, who had run the store for decades after immigrating to the United States and was well-known and liked throughout the neighborhood. The store was oddly quiet for the middle of a Saturday afternoon, and Stevens saw Giordano immediately: the heavyset man was sweeping a broom near the register at the front of the store. Giordano paused, turning to see who had come into his store. He ran a hand through his jet black hair, then rubbed his nose, his thick black mustache twitching.

"Good morning, Alexander!" he greeted, but Stevens noticed his smile seemed forced this morning. He saw the broken glass and overturned magazine rack. Then he realized that the till of the cash register was sitting open.

"Is everything all right, Mr. Giordano?" Stevens asked, concerned.

Giordano sighed heavily. "No, my boy," he said in thickly-accented but nevertheless understandable English, "it is not. Some hooligans just robbed me. They took all of the money that I had in the register."

"That's terrible, sir," Stevens said, earnestly. He stepped forward and lifted the magazine rack. "Here, let me help." After righting the magazine rack, he began to gather the magazines and comic books that had fallen to the floor when the rack was overturned.

"Who did this?" Stevens asked.

"Some of the boys in the neighborhood," Giordano replied, "who have fallen in with a bad element."

"I'm sorry," Stevens said.

"It is not your fault," Giordano said. "They need a better role model, I think. I hope that they are finding one soon. In the meantime, I recognized two of them. I will be speaking with their parents." He stopped sweeping and looked up at Stevens once again. "Please do not worry about this." He waved his hand, to indicate the broken glass and empty register. "No one was hurt. Now, what is it I can be doing for you?"

Stevens placed the last of the magazines and comic books back on the rack. He stood and brushed his hands on his pants, then smiled at Giordano. "I wanted to get a newspaper and a Coke," he said. "I haven't been able to keep up on the news very well, and I haven't had a Coke in a long time."

Giordano smiled. He walked to the cooler in the back corner of the store where the soft drinks were stored, to keep them cold. It had a glass door and was painted bright red with the Coca-Cola logo. He reached inside, pulled out a bottle, and quickly shut the cooler's glass door. Returning to the register, which was still open and empty, Giordano set the bottle, which was quickly gathering a sheen of condensation, on the counter and closed the till. He grabbed a copy of the *New York Post* from the stack near the register, and set it on the counter next to the bottle. He pulled out a bottle opener from under the counter, and popped the cap from the top of the Coke with a satisfying sound of escaping gas.

"How much do I owe you?" Stevens asked.

"Do not worry, my boy," Giordano replied.

"I can't do that," Stevens said. "You just got robbed."

"Everything will be all right," Giordano insisted.

Stevens knew that the Coke and the newspaper cost about five cents each. Giordano's generosity notwithstanding, he could not just take them. He reached into his pocket and pulled out a quarter. Leaving the coin on the counter as he took the drink and newspaper, he told the kindly older man, "Keep the change, sir. I insist."

Giordano smiled warmly at the younger man. He opened the register with a distinctive ring of a bell, and dropped the quarter into the till. "Thank you again, Alexander," Giordano said. "You are a good boy."

"Let me know if you need anything, Mr. Giordano," Stevens said. He turned and left the store. Taking a long drink from the Coke, Stevens stopped on the sidewalk in front of the store. He savored the taste and the sensation of the effervescent liquid as it rushed down his throat. It had been weeks since the last time he'd truly had an opportunity to indulge in a soft drink like this.

He sat on a bench nearby and took his time finishing the drink, savoring each sip until it was, finally, gone. He tossed the empty bottle into a trash can near the bench, then opened the newspaper and began to read. Just as with the copy of the *New York Times* that his father had been reading that morning, the newspaper was filled with depressing stories. It seemed overwhelming, and Stevens knew that there had to be something that he could do to make a difference in the world.

— § —

"Percy, are you all right? You've been awfully quiet," van Norton's mother asked as the family sat around the dinner table. The table itself was enormous, able to easily seat a dozen people, but only van Norton and his parents were using it this evening, and they sat at one end of the table together.

"Let him be, Margaret," his father said. "He's had a lot to process the last few days."

"I'm all right, mom," van Norton said. "Dad's right. I've just got a lot on my mind." He wanted to say more, but at the same time, he didn't want to upset his mother, and he knew that talking about what was on his mind, particularly how it related to his experiences in the war, would do exactly that.

"See?" his father interjected. "He's fine, dear."

Percy jabbed at his vegetables with his fork. After spearing several, he put the fork in his mouth and began to chew, slowly and deliberately. He was planning to meet with Stevens tomorrow in Central Park at noon. He had a feeling that, like him, his friend was having a similarly difficult transition after returning home.

CHAPTER FOUR

Stevens pulled the black ski mask down over his face. His eyes and mouth remained exposed, but it nevertheless sufficiently concealed his identity. He wore a black turtleneck, black pants, and his black combat boots. He pulled a pair of black gloves on to complete the outfit, and looked at himself in the mirror. It was no Superman costume, but it would do to keep his identity a secret from anyone who he might encounter.

He glanced once again at the door to his bedroom, and confirmed that the door was locked. He closed his eyes. He took a deep breath, held it for a moment, then let it out. He made a fist, held it up in front of him, and opened his eyes. For the first time since he had left Fort Leonard Wood, he activated his powers, like he had practiced hundreds of times in training. His fist began to glow, and even through his gloves, he could see the bones of his hand in the cloud of glowing plasma that surrounded his fist.

Willing the plasma to dissipate, he lowered his hand and pulled the mask from his head. He pulled his gloves off and unlocked his door. As he walked down the hallway toward the front door, he saw his parents in the living room, the television glowing faintly. His father looked up, and turned his head toward the hallway.

"Going somewhere, son?" his father asked.

"Out," Stevens said. "Maybe catch a movie."

"Jackie Gleason's on tonight," his father said, waving a hand toward the television set. "You're welcome to join us."

"That's all right," Stevens said. "Thank you."

"Have a good time," his father said.

"Thanks," Stevens said. "'Bye, dad. 'Bye, mom." He stepped through the front door, closing it quickly to keep the cold November air from blowing into the apartment. The stairway to the outside, despite being technically indoors, was still becoming quite cold at night. Earlier that month, a storm had brought more than two inches of snow and heavy winds, but the temperatures had risen back into the seventies during the day. Nights were still cold, though, and as Stevens stepped outside, he could see his breath escaping as a fog in the night air. He pulled the ski mask on, but kept it rolled up like a cap, and slipped on the gloves. He walked briskly down the street, then, after a couple of blocks, ducked out of sight down an alley. He pulled the mask down, looked around to make certain no one was around, then activated his powers.

His hands and feet glowed, plasma surrounding them. Concentrating, he focused his thoughts on where he wanted to go. He launched into the air, plasma billowing from his feet and hands. It was an amazing feeling of freedom: he was flying! Using the plasma from his hands to help guide the direction of his flight, he soared into the air over the roofs of the brownstones. He spun as he rose, corkscrewing through the air, then evened out his flight path and made his way across his neighborhood.

He began to head toward a part of town that he knew was prone to more criminal activity after night fell. He landed on a rooftop, and stood at the edge, quietly surveying the city before him. It didn't take long for him to hear muffled cries and curses.

Someone was being robbed. He launched himself back into the air, then dropped to the ground behind the obvious assailant. The victim, a dark-skinned woman bundled in warm clothing, was cowering against the wall in the alleyway. Her attacker, a large, imposing man in a leather coat, held a knife up in front of him, the blade pointing at the terrified woman. Her eyes became even wider and more terrified at the sight of Stevens dropping from the sky, his fists glowing with plasma. The assailant, so focused on his prey, didn't even seem to notice the crunch of Stevens' boots on the pavement as they hit the ground.

"Leave her alone," Stevens growled. The assailant turned around, surprised to hear a voice from behind him. His eyes widened further when he saw the plasma glowing around Stevens' hand. Before the assailant could react, the knife still held threateningly in his hand, Stevens punched the larger man in the jaw. The force of the blow, coupled with the shock of the plasma's energy, was more than enough, and the assailant dropped to the ground, unconscious. Stevens straightened up, his fist still glowing, and as he turned to the woman, she screamed and ran from the alley.

"You're welcome," Stevens muttered.

— § —

Stevens left the would-be mugger, seated and bound on the sidewalk at the entrance to the alleyway, and walked to a nearby payphone. He dropped a nickel into the slot and dialed.

"New York Police Department," a dainty, feminine voice answered after a single ring. "How can I direct your call?"

"I stopped a robbery," Stevens said. "I have the guy tied up. I need someone to come pick him up."

"I'll send a patrol car to you," the dispatcher said, surprised. "Please stay where you are." There was a brief pause, and the dispatcher asked, "Um, where are you?"

Stevens gave the cross streets. He hung up the phone, then walked back over to the would-be mugger. As he approached the larger man, he heard a muffled groan, and saw the would-be assailant's head start to move.

"Don't try to get up," Stevens said. "The police are on their way." As if on cue, the faint wail of a siren began to grow in the distance. Within moments, a large, black police car pulled up, its tires screeching to a halt as it arrived. The siren died down, though the light continued to strobe.

"Don't move!" a voice called out as a police officer jumped out of the passenger door of the police car. The officer was dressed in the heavy, high-collared, dark winter uniform of the New York Police Department, bright buttons running down either side of his torso, his badge shining on his left chest and atop the dark, high-peaked hat. His breath issued forth in clouds as he took aim with his service revolver.

Stevens put his hands up, palms facing the officer, to show that he wasn't a threat. "Easy, officer," he said as calmly as he could. "I'm on your side." The driver opened his door and stepped out of the car, his hand on the hilt of his revolver, which remained in its holster. He slowly walked toward the front of the vehicle, eyes darting between Stevens and the large, bound man on the sidewalk. "Like I told the lady on the phone, I caught this guy trying to rob an old woman. I knocked him out and tied him up for you."

"Where's the woman?" the driver asked. Stevens could hear a note of suspicion in his voice.

"She ran away," Stevens said. "She seemed pretty scared."

The driver looked more carefully at the bound man, his eyes narrowing. "Hey," he said after a moment, "I know you! Didn't I take you in for purse-snatching a few weeks ago? Up to your old tricks again?" The other officer lowered his weapon at last, and when he returned it to his holster, Stevens let his hands drop back to his sides. "Murphy," the driver said to his partner, "let's get our perp settled." The other officer, Murphy, moved toward the bound man, pulling out his handcuffs as he walked.

The driver, whose hand had moved away from his revolver after he recognized the suspect as someone he'd arrested before, now extended that hand toward Stevens. "Officer Patrick O'Grady," he said, introducing himself.

Stevens took the officer's hand and shook it. "A—" he began, then stopped himself. "*Nucleus.*"

Officer O'Grady's eyes narrowed. "Nucleus? That's kind of a funny name."

Stevens shrugged. "I, ah, I need to go. Now that you have this man in your custody."

O'Grady stiffened. "Now, hold on, I'm gonna need to take your statement."

"I gave it to you," Nucleus insisted.

"And I'm gonna need a *name* to go with that statement," O'Grady continued.

"I'm," Stevens tried not to stammer, "I'm Nucleus."

"Sir," O'Grady's voice became firm. "Take off the mask, please."

"I have to go," Nucleus said. He activated his powers, and shot into the night sky. O'Grady and Murphy stared up in shock and amazement as he receded into the darkness.

"Holy mother of God," Murphy muttered.

— § —

Sunday, November 22, 1953

Stevens sat on a bench in Central Park, a copy of the *New York Daily Bulletin* in his hands. As he paged through the newspaper, he couldn't find anything on the crime that he had stopped the night before, but there was still plenty of bad news to go around: a fifteen-year-old girl had been killed by a stray bullet, the smog that had engulfed Brooklyn all week wasn't expected to lift anytime soon, there was an attempted hijacking of a shipment of women's clothing, and half the paper seemed to be stories about communism: it was being blamed for a rise in antisemitism, communist infiltration was being brought up in the run-up to the 1954 presidential campaign, riots in communist countries...

Stevens was reading a story about an appropriations bill being proposed by Senator Jaspar Crow when he heard someone clear their throat nearby.

"So that's where you disappeared to," Percy van Norton said, grinning. "I've been trying to find you for almost twenty minutes!"

Stevens folded the newspaper and set it on the bench. Rising, he took van Norton's hand with a smile. "Good to see you, van Norton."

"We're not in the military anymore," van Norton said. "I think it's all right if you call me Percy now."

"In that case," Stevens agreed, "call me Alex."

The two shook hands, grinning. "Alex it is," van Norton said.

Stevens tossed the newspaper into a nearby trash can as the pair began to walk down the path, away from the bench. After several moments, van Norton broke the silence. "How have you been adjusting?"

"Oh, you know," Stevens hedged, "just trying to find my place again."

"That bad, eh?" van Norton asked. Stevens grimaced, and van Norton added assuringly, "Don't feel too bad. I'm in the same boat." Stevens looked at him askance, not quite believing his wealthy friend. "No, really. I have everything I could want, sure, but I don't feel like I've really *earned* it. That's something I never would have even thought about before the war."

"I feel like there's so much *more* that I could be doing," Stevens said. "All the crime, and the corruption out there..."

"And with our powers," van Norton picked up the thought, then left it hanging for Stevens to continue.

"And with our powers," Stevens repeated, "we could really *do* something about it."

"You want to be a superhero," van Norton sighed. "I *knew* it. It was only a matter of time. Somebody would end up doing it."

"I stopped a robbery last night," Stevens admitted. "A purse snatching." He sighed. His shoulders drooped, and his head sagged. "The woman was terrified of me. She ran away screaming. The police almost shot me when they showed up."

"Guy with glowing fists," van Norton said, an amused expression crossing his face. "I can see how that might make people nervous."

"I think it was more than that," Stevens began, then paused, collecting his thoughts. "I think it was how I was dressed."

"How you were *dressed?*" van Norton asked, confused.

"I was trying to protect my identity," Stevens admitted, "like Batman or Captain America. I had a ski mask on... and I was wearing black."

Van Norton tried not to laugh, but was only partially successful. He chuckled as he said, "You looked like a bad guy, you mean."

Stevens covered his face in his hand. "Yeah," he admitted.

They walked in silence for almost a full minute before van Norton spoke. "I," he hesitated. "I might be able to help with that."

"What do you mean?" Stevens asked.

"I know some people, who know some people," van Norton said. "I can get you a cost—" he stopped, then corrected himself, "a *uniform*."

Stevens looked at him in surprise. "You're okay with this?"

"I don't know," van Norton admitted. "I feel like I need to do something, too. Maybe this can be my way of helping."

"I don't know what to say," Stevens admitted.

"You could start with 'thank you,'" van Norton teased.

"Thank you," Stevens said, seriously.

"This could take a while," van Norton warned. "Getting a superhero... uniform and keeping it quiet means it will take longer than just getting a suit made."

"I understand," Stevens said. "I'm ready to get started."

"I'll introduce you to one of my tailors, then," van Norton said. "He knows how to be... discreet."

CHAPTER FIVE

Saturday, December 19, 1953

Percy van Norton handed a package to Alex Stevens. It was wrapped in brown paper, and tied with thin twine. The pair were standing in a large room at the van Norton estate in the Bronx. Stevens guessed it must be a library or a study of some sort, as the walls were lined with bookshelves.

"Thanks," Stevens said as he took the package. The paper crinkled softly in his hands as he turned it over, absentmindedly examining the wrapped package.

Van Norton indicated a couch flanked by a pair of overstuffed chairs nearby. They occupied the center of the room, with a small table in front of them, atop a relatively modest, fringed rug. Lamps sat on small end tables at either end of the couch, between it and the chairs, forming a curved seating area that faced an enormous window that gave an impressive view of the estate grounds outside. Through the window, Stevens could see the trees that lined the estate, forming a natural barrier between the van Nortons and their neighbors, and large, grassy areas with stone paths, outdoor furniture, and more luxury than he had experienced in his entire life. Beyond the trees, the Manhattan skyline was visible in the distance.

The men sat on the couch, and Stevens unwrapped the package that his friend had given to him. Inside, he saw bright, durable cloth. He lifted the garment, examining it. It was a yellow top and pants that would be tight and form-fitting when worn. He'd told van Norton that he gave the police "Nucleus" as his name; his mind had blanked, and it was the first thing he could think of besides his actual name. Using that as his superheroic identity, they had developed a symbol like Superman or Batman wore on their chests: a stylized, black radiation symbol enclosed in a circle. The suit was accompanied by a large piece of heavy blue cloth—the cape—and a pair of matching blue gloves and blue trunks, folded underneath the suit. As Stevens felt the smooth material, van Norton pulled out a bag that he'd set down next to the couch earlier. He handed the bag to Stevens, and said, "Merry Christmas."

Stevens set the suit on the table in front of him and took the bag from van Norton. He pulled out a pair of boots. They were tall and had no laces or buckles, and the leather was dyed a shade of blue that matched the rest of the uniform. There was also a leather domino mask in the bag, also dyed blue, and a small bottle with an amber liquid inside, and a brush visible within, apparently attached to the inside of the lid. Stevens lifted the mask to his face, and it fit perfectly. That explained why the tailor had taken a plaster cast of his face during the fitting for the outfit. There was also a leather belt, again dyed blue, with a golden buckle to complete the ensemble.

"That's spirit gum," van Norton explained, indicating the bottle. "It'll hold the mask to your face, and I'm told that it won't hurt too much when you take it off. There's some black makeup—don't laugh—in the bag. You put that around your eyes before you put the mask on, to help blend it with your face. That will help conceal your identity."

"Maybe I should try this on," Stevens said. "See how it looks."

"There's a bathroom two doors down the hall on the right," van Norton offered. Stevens gathered the clothing and put everything into the bag with the boots. Carrying it in the crook of his left arm—he was still accustomed to keeping his right hand free at all times, a habit developed in the military in case he ever needed to salute someone—he made his way down the hall and into the bathroom. This house—this *mansion*—was enormous. The library he and van Norton had been in was nearly half the size of his parents' apartment in Brooklyn, and it was just one of dozens of rooms here, and not even remotely close to being the largest of them. Van Norton had grown up thinking of this as normal; everything must have come as such a shock to him when he was drafted.

Stepping into the bathroom, he closed the door behind him and turned the latch, locking the door. Setting the bag on the counter—yes, there was a counter, and this bathroom was almost as large as his bedroom—he began to disrobe. Once he'd stripped down to his socks and underwear, he pulled out the uniform from the bag. He pulled the pants and top on, then the trunks.

Sitting on the edge of the toilet, he pulled on the boots, then stood and returned to the rest of the items on the counter. He unfurled the cape with a snap, then spun it around to his back. It had hidden buckles that attached it to his shoulders, and he fastened them. The cape flowed from his shoulders, and hung past his waist, just past the end of the trunks. He was glad that it wasn't too long, as he didn't want to have to risk tripping on the cape while he was out and acting as a superhero.

Stevens laid out the black makeup container, the bottle of spirit gum, and the mask. Hesitantly, he opened the makeup container, then used the small cloth pad within to apply a small amount of the thick makeup to his eyelids, then spread it around the orbits of his eyes. Satisfied, he set that down, then opened the bottle of spirit gum. It had the slightly bitter scent of alcohol. Using the brush, he applied it to the inside of the mask, coating the interior surface as best he could. He screwed the cap back onto the bottle, then lifted the mask to his face. He pressed it into place, holding it steady for a moment. He wasn't sure how long it would take for the adhesive to take hold, so he held the mask firmly against his face for several seconds. Tentatively, he pulled his fingers away, and the mask held firm.

He picked up the belt, then threaded it through the loops on the trunks. Making sure that the top was thoroughly tucked in, he tightened the belt, then picked up the gloves. He put them on, and, at long last, inspected his reflection in the full-length mirror installed on the wall near the door.

Once he was satisfied that everything appeared to be in order, he folded his clothes and put them into the bag. Leaving the bag on the counter, he unlocked the bathroom door, opened it, and stepped into the hallway. He paused a moment, then walked toward the study where van Norton was waiting for him. Hearing the soft click of the boot heels on the hardwood floor, van Norton rose from the couch and turned toward the open doorway.

"Jesus," van Norton muttered, "you look like a comic book."

Stevens shrugged. "That's the point," he said. "If I'm going to be a superhero and try not to get shot by the good guys, I need to look the part."

"You ready to go out and fight the good fight?" van Norton asked.

Stevens cocked his head, his eyes narrowing. "Now?" he asked.

"Why not?" van Norton replied. "No time like the present."

— § —

Stevens—*Nucleus*—shot into the sky, his cape billowing in the rush of wind as he corkscrewed through the air. He flew up into the clouds, then shot above them. He slowed his ascent, hanging briefly in the air as the thrust he was generating with his plasma was momentarily equal to the force of gravity, then began to fall. He turned his body into the fall, turning it into a dive. He stretched his fists before him, and angled himself south, toward Manhattan.

The wind continued to whip past him, and he picked up speed as he fell. The feeling was incredible, and he couldn't help but grin widely. It didn't take long for him to reach the tops of the skyscrapers, and he continued to race through the sky over the city, dropping like a stone. As he flew nearer to the ground, he began to see the shapes of people. Someone had noticed him, as people were stopping, looking up at him, and pointing. He spread his arms, palms out, and began to apply reverse thrust to slow his speed and change his angle of descent. He leveled out somewhere around three or four stories above the ground, and shot over the heads of the amazed crowd below.

It didn't take long to find a crime to stop. He saw a car swerving through traffic, a police car in pursuit. Someone was leaning out of the passenger window of the car, and was firing a pistol at the pursuing police cruiser. Nucleus' eyes narrowed, and he picked up speed to overtake the car. *Someone could be hurt or killed by those stray bullets,* he thought. *I have to stop them!* He fired a blast of plasma at the rear wheel of the car as he shot past. The tire exploded, and the driver struggled to regain control of the vehicle as it began to fishtail wildly.

The man with the gun pulled himself back inside just as the driver hit the curb. The car jumped the curb, then flipped onto the driver's side and began to roll, stopping only when it slammed into another car traveling in the opposite direction. Nucleus circled back, and landed on the pavement near the overturned car at virtually the same time as the police cruiser came to a stop. A crowd gathered nearby, and Nucleus could hear the distinctive clicking sound as someone started to snap photographs of the scene.

The police officers exited their vehicle. One ran toward the over-turned car, his revolver drawn and ready, while the other cautiously approached Nucleus. His expression serious, he held his left hand out, fingers splayed as if to say, "stop right there," and his right hand hovered near the revolver in its holster at his hip.

Nucleus held his hands out, to show he wasn't a threat. "I'm on your side, officer," he said. "I'm just here to help."

"Someone could have been killed," the officer replied, "with that stunt you just pulled."

"And all those stray bullets they were shooting," Nucleus countered, "would hurt or kill even more people. That chase was endangering hundreds of people. I had the power to stop it, and I did." The police officer tensed. *Well,* Nucleus thought, *maybe that wasn't the best way to put that.* "I'm on your side, officer," he said again, his hands out to his sides, as non-threateningly as possible. "I'm just here to help."

One of the people with cameras broke through the front line of the gathered crowd. He wore a dark gray business suit, a black tie, and a fedora at an odd angle. He paused for a moment, raised his camera to his face, and the flashbulb exploded once again. Nucleus had turned to see what the commotion was all about, and happened to be looking directly at the camera when the bulb went off. Temporarily blinded, with spots clouding his vision, Nucleus blinked and realized that the odd angle of the hat was due to the camera's large flash assembly pushing against it every time the man raised the camera to his face.

As his vision began to clear, Nucleus saw the man was moving his way. "Harry Sanders, *New York Daily Bulletin,*" he announced, pulling out a press pass and holding it out like a talisman. He looked at Nucleus. "Who are you?"

Nucleus was expecting this question, but it was still a somewhat daunting moment. "Nucleus," he said. "Call me Nucleus." Before the reporter could ask any further questions, he looked back at the police officer he'd been speaking with. "If you'll excuse me," he said, "I have to be going now." He activated his powers, and took off into the sky.

—$—

As Nucleus soared over the skies of New York, he recalled the incident with Mr. Giordano's shop the day after he'd returned home. Some of the neighborhood boys "who have fallen in with a bad element," as Giordano had put it, were robbing stores and causing trouble throughout the neighborhood. The older shopkeeper had also said that "they need a better role model."

Maybe it was a terrible idea, but maybe he could be that role model. Nucleus realized that he had been flying for several minutes without really paying attention to where he was going. As he regained his bearings, he realized that he was very close to his neighborhood. Maybe it was fate.

He lowered his altitude, and found a rooftop with a good vantage point. He landed with the soft crunch of gravel under his boots, and walked to the corner of the building, where he could take in the best view of the surrounding area. It didn't take long for him to find a group of teenage boys gathered near one of the brownstones. Taking a deep breath to steel his nerves, he launched himself into the air, then made a dramatic landing near the boys.

"Boys," he said warmly as he landed. Most of them looked awestruck at the sight of an honest-to-God superhero landing on their street. One of the boys seemed more jaded. His arms crossed over his chest, each hand held onto the opposite arm of his black leather jacket.

"Who are you supposed to be?" he asked, a faint sneer in his voice.

"Yeah!" one of the younger boys chimed in.

"You can call me Nucleus," he introduced himself. "I was... patrolling the city, and I thought I'd introduce myself."

The apparent leader's eyes narrowed in suspicion. "Why's that?"

"Just your friendly, neighborhood superhero making his debut tonight," Nucleus said. "I wanted to get off on the right foot. Say my hellos, stop some bad guys, that sort of thing."

"Right," the leader said. "You said hello, old man. Now you can say goodbye."

"Excuse me?" Nucleus asked.

"You heard me," the boy said. "You're on our turf. We don't need you, we don't want you. You can go, or we can make you go." He flicked open a switchblade knife. "Your choice."

Nucleus stood straighter. This was not going how he'd hoped it would go. "That's not necessary," he began.

The leader laughed, and turned halfway to address the boys in his gang. "He's just as yellow as his stupid costume!" The other boys began to laugh, nervously at first, then more confidently as the group began laughing together.

"I don't want to fight kids," Nucleus protested. "I don't want to hurt anyone."

"Only one gonna get hurt," the leader said menacingly, "is you."

Nucleus sighed. This *really* wasn't going the way he'd hoped. "Son," he said, "this is not a good move for you." He charged up the plasma in his right fist. It began to glow, and the other boys' eyes widened.

The leader lunged forward in a sloppy attack. Nucleus easily dodged the blow. He let his power dissipate; he wouldn't need it to take down this amateur hour thug. As the hand holding the knife sailed past his chest, Nucleus grabbed the wrist in an iron grip with his left hand. He spun, pinning the boy's arm at the elbow with his own arm and side. With his right elbow, he delivered a blow to the boy's solar plexus, knocking the wind out of him. The boy lost his grip on the knife, which clattered to the pavement. In one fluid motion, Nucleus kicked it aside, spun, then hooked his leg behind the boy's ankles and kicked. The youth, already off-balance, fell to the ground with a thud, followed by a smacking sound from the back of his head striking the pavement.

Nucleus stood, looking down at the teenage boy with delusions of manhood. He was unconscious, probably from the blow to the head from hitting the pavement, but otherwise unhurt. He crossed his arms, and raised one hand to his face, closing his eyes and shaking his head. "Jesus, kid," he muttered. "That was incredibly stupid." He looked up, and saw the other boys were staring, wide-eyed and open-mouthed, at the scene before them.

"Go home, kids," he said. "Find another leader." He indicated the unconscious boy on the pavement at his feet. "This guy is only going to lead you into trouble." The boy at his feet began to stir, then moaned. Nucleus looked down as the boys began to disperse. "It's over, kid," Nucleus said. "Go home. Do something better with your life."

Nucleus stepped away, then launched himself into the sky. The sun was setting, and it was beginning to look like the makings of a beautiful evening.

Chapter Six

Wednesday, December 23, 1953

röhe Weinachten, Mein Herr," Erich Eidelmann said in greeting as he approached the older man seated at the desk that dominated the room. Eidelmann wore plain clothing, but his well-muscled build was nevertheless apparent through the loose clothing, and his hair was just as blond as it had been in his youth. The benefit of strong genes. *Superior genes,* he corrected himself.

"Merry Christmas to you as well, my boy," the older man replied. "To what do I owe the pleasure of your visit?"

"*Herr* Schmachenberg," Eidelmann began, "today is my nineteenth birthday. I wish to serve the Reich—"

"The Reich no longer exists," Schmachenberg interrupted bitterly. "You were but a boy, but you were there. You remember."

"Yes, *Mein Herr,* I remember," Eidelmann said. "But as long as we remain, so too does the Reich. We can rebuild it, make it even grander than ever!"

Schmachenberg snorted. "Such youthful exuberance. There are but a few thousand of us. We would not stand a chance against even one of the minor military powers as we are now."

"I disagree," Eidelmann protested.

"Your... *freakish* abilities," Schmachenberg replied disdainfully, "would not provide enough of an edge to be of any great import." His eyes narrowed, and he glared across the desk at Eidelmann. "Were your parents not who they were, and were you otherwise not so perfectly Aryan, I would have had you put down as soon as those abilities surfaced."

"Perhaps it is *because* I am so perfectly Aryan," Eidelmann countered, "that I have these abilities at all."

Schmachenberg guffawed. "Hardly, boy," he replied, then sighed. "This is an old argument, and we will not solve it today. You have a plan, I take it?"

"I will take a force of our finest *Sturmtruppen,*" Eidelmann said, "and attack the American capitol. We will cut off the head of the snake, and claim America in the name of the Reich."

"And you will die," Schmachenberg replied. "And so will every man under your command." He looked at the younger man with a mixture of pity and disgust. "A few hundred soldiers, at best, against the heart of the American defense? Have you learned nothing?"

"You suggest another target?" Eidelmann asked.

"If I were to make such a suggestion," Schmachenberg said, "it would certainly be for a location less well defended, yet still highly visible. But I make no such suggestion. Your plan is foolhardy."

"What would you have us do?" Eidelmann asked. "Rot here for another ten years? Twenty? *Fifty?* What of our duty to restore the Reich—"

"None of that matters if we are all killed in foolish battles!" Schmachenberg snapped. "We do not have the manpower. This means we must have superior technology to make up for our numbers. I have had my scientists working tirelessly to this end. We must be patient. Victory goes to the prepared."

"As you say, *Mein Herr,*" Eidelmann conceded bitterly. He knew there was no convincing Schmachenberg, but he had to try. After his parents had died of malaria a year ago, Schmachenberg, the highest ranking of the former Nazi officials and generals, had taken de facto control of the community. He made no secret that he considered the emergence of superpowered humans an affront to the Nazi ideals of genetic purity and superiority, and he placed far more confidence in technology than people... particularly superhuman people.

As his parents and several others in the community became ill, news began to creep in from the outside world about the growing number of people known to have super powers appearing throughout the world, and Eidelmann's own powers began to manifest. He soon discovered that he could summon—and later generate—lightning bolts, and with a great deal of concentration, he had begun to teach himself how to levitate. It was his hope that he would soon be able to fly.

"With your permission," Eidelmann said. Schmachenberg nodded, no longer even looking at Eidelmann. He raised his arm and waved his hand dismissively from the wrist. Eidelmann came to attention, snapped the heels of his boots together, and gave a half bow from the waist. He returned to the position of attention, spun on his heel in an about-face, and marched for the door to Schmachenberg's office. What had been his father's office until he fell ill.

Making his way outside, Eidelmann fumed. Schmachenberg had such tunnel vision, refusing to see the advantage that superhuman powers gave their cause, and refusing to see that they were the next step forward in the evolution of the Aryan race. He would show the old coward. He would gather the forces loyal to him, and he would carry out his plans, parts of which had already been put into motion.

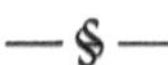

"Who is this man?" the elderly Chinese man asked, tapping his finger on the photograph of Nucleus on the front page of the newspaper spread out on the table before him. The elderly man, Chen Chang, sat at the head of a large table with several younger men, all Chinese. While the younger men wore western business suits, Chang wore traditional Chinese robes made of a deep, silken red cloth. Smoke snaked into the air from burning incense holders placed around the room.

"They call him Nucleus," one of the younger men said, deferently. He wore a well-pressed black suit with a white shirt and black necktie. A pair of horn-rimmed glasses obscured his eyes.

"I know that," Chang snapped. "I am not illiterate. That does not tell me who he *is*."

"We," the younger man began to sputter, "we don't know who he really is." He stiffened in his seat and bowed his head in shame.

"Then I suggest that you find out," Chang said. "He is beginning to interfere in our operations, and I want him removed from the picture."

— $ —

Friday, December 25, 1953

"Merry Christmas, Alex," Evelyn said as she handed a package to Stevens. It was wrapped in metallic green foil, and tied with a thick, red ribbon. She had come over to the Stevens' apartment that morning, to join with the family in their holiday gift-giving.

Smiling at her as he took the gift, he replied, "Merry Christmas." He inspected it for a moment, appreciating the wrapping paper, then ripped into the package with a satisfying sound of tearing paper. "What's this?" he asked. "A shirt?" To his surprise, it wasn't a box of clothing like he'd expected. Instead, the word "Scrabble" was emblazoned in large, bold letters on the top of the box.

"I thought that would be something we could do together," Evelyn said.

"That sounds great," Stevens agreed. "Thanks." He turned in his seat on the sofa next to Evelyn, then set the box on top of the small pile of gifts that he had collected.

"This one's for Evelyn," Stevens' younger sister, Megan, singsonged from where she sat on the floor by the tree. Megan had recently graduated from high school, and was working as a secretary in an office in Manhattan. She had brown hair like her father and brother, but otherwise had inherited her mother's features. She held a small box wrapped in plain, red wrapping paper, holding the tag so that she could read it. She stood and leaned over so that she could hand the small box to Evelyn, who held out her hand and leaned forward in her seat to accept the gift.

Evelyn tore the paper delicately and carefully, revealing a small, leather jewelry box with a hinged lid. Opening the box, she found a delicate silver necklace and matching earrings inside. She turned to Stevens and embraced him.

"Thank you," she said. "I love it."

Chapter Seven

Monday, December 28, 1953

Nucleus dropped to the pavement behind a warehouse near the docks. He moved cautiously, trying to minimize the sound of his footsteps. It was late evening, and the night was dark. The moon was in its last quarter; the shadows were deep and dark. He clung to them, cautiously looking around corners as he made his way between the warehouses and through the dock yards.

The docks were sparsely populated, due to the late hour, though there was still constant work to be done. Nucleus made good use of his training in evasion techniques from the Marine Corps, and despite the bright colors he wore, he went unnoticed as he made his way down the rows of warehouses. It was slow going, but he'd attract too much attention if he flew straight there.

Word on the street was that one of the Chinese gangs was bringing in a massive shipment of opium. He'd spent two days chasing leads, and it had led him here, tonight. Arriving at the warehouse he sought, he buried himself in the shadows of the alleyway behind the building that serviced it and the other warehouses on the row. He looked around cautiously, confirming that no one was watching him, and flew a few feet into the air, grabbing at the emergency ladder that dangled above his head. The shadows vanished for a moment as his powers illuminated the alleyway around him, but it couldn't be helped; he only hoped that by minimizing it like he had, he would continue to go unnoticed.

Nucleus climbed the ladders in the dark until he reached a doorway near the roof. He grabbed the knob, but when he tried to turn it, he found that the door was locked. He had expected that to be the case, but he had hoped it wouldn't be. Shielding the door from view with his body as much as he could, Nucleus pushed his right index finger into the key slot on the knob. Concentrating all of his power into that fingertip, he delivered a blast that melted the lock mechanism in the doorknob. He tested the knob again, and it turned easily.

Slipping through the now-open doorway, Nucleus shut the door behind himself, trying to eliminate as much evidence from outside eyes that he was there, or that he had passed through that way. He found himself on a grated catwalk, suspended dozens of feet in the air above the warehouse floor below. The lights were on, but in such a cavernous structure, there was still quite a bit of shadow to conceal him. He could hear muffled voices in the distance ahead. Making his way cautiously forward, Nucleus saw a group of men gathered around two large shipping containers. They seemed to be arguing, but Nucleus couldn't understand what they were saying. The language sounded in some ways like the Korean he'd heard during the war, but in other ways it sounded completely alien to his ears. *They must be speaking in Chinese*, he decided. He had no idea what they were arguing about. Where to put those containers, perhaps?

He watched for about a minute or two, assessing the scene before him. This was the right warehouse. This was the right time. There was a group of people speaking Chinese, with a pair of large shipping containers in the dead of night. The information he'd managed to gather seemed to have paid off. The men didn't seem to be armed as far as he could tell, but it was always possible that they had pistols concealed under their coats; best to assume they were, so he wouldn't be surprised if someone pulled a gun on him once he made his appearance. He scanned the area, and spotted a good spot to land and make his grand entrance: it gave him a clear view of all of the men around the crates, and provided some cover in case they pulled guns and he needed to avoid getting shot.

Okay, he thought, *now or never*. He climbed over the railing on the side of the catwalk, then let himself fall. At the last moment, he activated his powers, decelerating to land safely, and with a bright, splashy, potentially intimidating effect on top of it all. One of the men shouted something in Chinese and pulled a gun from inside his jacket. I hate being right all the time, Nucleus thought. Then another pulled a gun. And another. Within moments, every single one of the Chinese men had a gun pointed in his direction. Nucleus dove for the cover he'd spotted, a medium-sized crate. Wood splinters flew through the air as bullets cracked against the crate's opposite side.

This was a trap! They'd been waiting for him! He looked around. There was no way he could reach any of the doors without taking a round. *No exfiltration plan,* he chided himself. *Great move, idiot. Okay. Think.* There were four men, apparently all armed. All had pistols, so magazine capacity was limited. They had already stopped firing, probably to reload, and were shouting something in Chinese. It wouldn't be long before they started to advance on his position, so...

Nucleus leaped to his feet, turning to face his opponents. Extending his arms as he rose, he unleashed a torrent of plasma in their direction, making it as energetic as he could, and it shot out like lightning. Just as quickly, he returned to cover behind the crate. The hail of gunfire started once again, as well as another sound. Pounding? It almost sounded like someone pounding on one of the wooden crates. Just as the gunfire stopped once again, there was a sound of wood cracking and splintering, then clattering to the ground. Someone had opened a crate, but for what?

Nucleus rose once again, and paused momentarily in disbelief at the sight that greeted him. The two large crates were now open, their sides facing him shattered, the wood splintered on the ground... from the inside out. The four men had been joined by nearly a dozen more, and at least four of the new arrivals had rifles. They were taking no chances on this trap, and he needed to find a way out of here. *Now.*

Diving for cover once more, he looked around. Inspiration struck him when he finally looked up. There was an enormous lamp, practically a stadium spotlight, hanging from the ceiling almost directly above the men and the now-empty crates. Nucleus charged up his fist, collecting as much energy into the plasma blast as he could before he threw it. He jumped up and unleashed the plasma at the cable that held the lamp to the ceiling. As he did so, he felt a sharp pressure in his left bicep. He returned to cover as the lamp crashed to the ground, crushing the other men underneath it. He shot into the air toward the door he'd come in through. Someone hadn't gotten caught underneath, because he could hear more gunshots and even heard one bullet zip through the air past his ear.

But he made it through the door. His arm was really starting to hurt. He glanced down, and saw a growing red stain on his left bicep. He'd been shot, but he needed to get to safety before he could do anything about it. He shot into the night sky, not worrying about stealth any longer. He flew to the end of the docks, and landed on the roof of a nearby building. His heart was racing, his adrenaline was spiking, and his breathing was ragged.

He looked around. Someone in this building had left their wash out to dry on a line and had apparently forgotten to bring it in at the end of the day. He grabbed a sock, wrapped it around his upper arm, and tied the ends together. The pain intensified for a moment, then ebbed back to a dull, fiery ache. *That should stop the bleeding*, he thought.

Nucleus knew that he had to get this treated. But how? Where? He couldn't just walk into a hospital, dressed like this. If he changed clothes, that might raise questions about why there was no bullet wound on the sleeve. And then there was the question of how he'd pay the bill for that. His wound dressed, at least temporarily, he looked north, toward the Bronx. Van Norton might be able to help. At any rate, he didn't know who else he could turn to.

— § —

"Fortunately, the bullet passed cleanly through the bicep," the doctor said as he examined Nucleus' arm. Nucleus was resting on a lushly-appointed bed in one of the many guest rooms in the van Norton estate. He'd removed the cape, top, and boots of his uniform, but his mask was still in place. Van Norton trusted the doctor, but Nucleus didn't know him, and was hesitant to potentially expose his identity unless he had to. "Keep the wound clean, and it should heal nicely over the next three weeks."

Nucleus sighed in relief, then winced as the doctor began to force water through the wound, which collected into a red puddle in a ceramic basin placed under his arm, which in turn sat atop several layers of towels that protected the bed sheets. He applied a generous amount of a white powdery substance to the wound; sulfa, he guessed. Once cleaned and sterilized, the doctor began to wrap the wound in bandages, with gauze pads on both the entrance and exit wounds. He discussed treatment and wound care with Nucleus, never once asking questions like "How did this happen?" or "Who are you?" He then cleaned up the basin, towels, and other medical debris. When he was finished, he smiled, shook Nucleus' hand, and stood from his seat next to the bed.

"Thank you, doctor," van Norton said, rising from his own chair. He joined the doctor, and the two shook hands before van Norton guided the doctor out. After a couple of minutes, van Norton returned to the room, closing the doors behind him.

"You are incredibly lucky, Alex," van Norton said, seriously, after a moment. He sat on the end of the bed, next to Nucleus' feet, and looked his friend in the eyes.

"No kidding," Nucleus agreed.

"You're staying here tonight," van Norton declared.

"What?" Nucleus asked, incredulous. "It's late, Percy. I have to get home—"

"I already called," van Norton said. "I told your family that we met up this evening and that I invited you to stay here. Apparently they think I'm helping you look for a job."

Nucleus groaned. His job hunt had stalled weeks ago, partly due to the holidays. Yet another thing he didn't want to think about at the moment.

Van Norton chuckled. "I really can help you with that," he said. "For now, get changed, and get some rest. I had some pajamas and clothes in your size brought up when you were in and out of consciousness earlier."

Nucleus blinked. "Uh, thanks," he said.

Van Norton clapped a hand on Nucleus' shin. "It's the least I can do for a friend," van Norton said, smiling. Seriously, he added, "You're one of the only real friends I've got, Alex." He stood up again, turning to keep his attention focused on Nucleus. "Get some rest. I'll see you in the morning." Van Norton returned to the doors, which he closed once again as he left the room.

Nucleus rose from the bed and walked over to the small table where the clothing and some towels had been placed. He stripped down to his underwear, then put on the pajamas. They seemed to be silk, or at least something very much like it. Whatever the material, they were incredibly smooth and luxurious to the touch. He realized that he was still wearing the mask, and peeled it away from his face, then he left the room and walked down the hallway until he found the bathroom. Taking a washcloth and some soap, he cleaned off the black makeup from around his eyes, and discovered that there was a new toothbrush and tube of toothpaste sitting next to the sink. He brushed his teeth, then made his way back to the bedroom. It didn't take long for him to fall asleep.

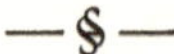

Stevens woke with a start. It took several panicked seconds for him to remember that he was in a guest room at the van Norton estate, and how he'd gotten there. Then his thoughts were able to dwell on the dream.

The *nightmare.*

Before, the dreams—the *nightmares*—had been about combat and the battles he'd fought in during the war. This was a new one. This was different. This was about what had happened last night, except it had ended very differently than what had really happened. This was his mind replaying that disaster, and throwing in the worst-case scenario of just how badly it could have gone. There but for the grace of God go I, Stevens thought, darkly.

Stevens examined the room around him. It was still dark; the sun clearly had not yet risen. What time was it? He couldn't find a clock anywhere. Was it late enough that he should just stay up and wait for sunrise, or should he try to go back to bed?

He got out of bed and began to roam the room. He stopped at the large window. The soft glow of moonlight reflected off of snow filtered into the room. It seemed to be the middle of the night still, given how high in the sky the moon still was, and he still felt exhausted. He decided that he would go back to sleep, but discovered that, after that nightmare, sleep did not return so easily.

CHAPTER EIGHT
Tuesday, January 19, 1954

Stevens sat in the comfortable armchair in his parents' living room. The television set was on, tuned to a local news broadcast, casting a pale glow in the otherwise darkened room. His parents sat together on the sofa with his sister, Megan, and the family watched the screen together.

"...been three weeks," the news anchor, a well-groomed man with dark hair and a dark suit, said from the television screen, "and still no sign of Nucleus, the world's first superhero." The camera panned down toward the desk and zoomed in, where the news anchor held up a photograph of Nucleus. "He made a splash last month, stopping a pair of bank robbers who were being pursued by police just two days before Christmas. After a week of highly visible heroics, Nucleus just as suddenly disappeared from public view. The question remains on everyone's minds: where did he go?"

"Probably got himself killed," Stevens' father muttered. Stevens' mother squirmed uncomfortably at hearing the macabre thought given voice.

"What was that, daddy?" Megan asked, leaning forward in her seat on the opposite end of the sofa and looking at him.

"Nothing, sweetheart," he replied. Now it was Stevens' turn to shift uncomfortably in his seat. "Everything all right, son?" his father asked, looking at him through narrowed, curious eyes.

"Yes, sir," he managed not to stammer in reply. "I—I just hope Nucleus is all right."

"I'm sure he is," his father replied. "He's a superhero, right? Like in those comic books you used to read when you were a kid."

"Yes, sir," Stevens said. "But life isn't a comic book."

"No, son, it is not," his father agreed.

— § —

"I hope he doesn't come back," Evelyn said as she shared lunch with Stevens the next day at a small diner in their neighborhood.

Stevens gave her a confused look. "Who?" he asked.

"Nucleus," she practically spat the name. The shocked look must have been evident on his face. "Oh, I hope he wasn't killed or something," she explained. "We just... we have enough problems in this world without having to worry about costumed do-gooders running around, with their freaky superpowers and ridiculous outfits." She paused, scowling. "He's probably a commie, too."

Stevens suddenly found that he had lost his appetite. He set his fork down on his plate, and just stared at it for a moment. He couldn't bring himself to look up at Evelyn just yet. It was so... *surreal* for her to love him and hate him at the same time, even if she didn't know that's what was happening. "I don't think he's a communist," was all he could bring himself to say.

"Okay, maybe he's not a commie," Evelyn conceded. "But we don't need superheroes in real life. We got police for that kind of thing. And comic books rot your brains. There's this psychiatrist, he said comic books cause juvenile delinquency! This guy's probably one of them delinquents!"

"If he were a delinquent," Stevens countered, "why would he be *stopping* criminals?"

"There's just something about him I don't like," Evelyn admitted. "Why the mask? Why all the secrets? What's he got to hide?"

"Maybe he's trying to protect the people close to him," Stevens offered.

"That's not a problem for the police," Evelyn replied. "They don't hide behind masks. And why are you defending him so hard? You soft on him or something?"

"I think he's trying to do the right thing," Stevens said, trying to hold in just how uncomfortable and angry he was becoming. "And there's a lot of police. There's only one of him." Evelyn scowled and looked at her plate.

"I think I lost my appetite," she said after a moment.

The pair sat in uncomfortable silence for several moments before Stevens said, "Me too."

The silence continued for several more seconds. Evelyn began to gather her belongings. "Maybe I should go," she said at last.

"I'll get the check," Stevens said. "I'll see you later, okay?"

Evelyn's features softened. She smiled, but even Stevens could tell it was forced. "Okay," she agreed. She stood up from the table, leaned over, and gave him a quick kiss on the cheek. Then she turned and walked briskly from the diner.

— $ —

"How's the arm?" Percy van Norton asked Stevens once they had settled into the overstuffed armchairs of the... library? Study? *I should probably ask what this room is,* Stevens thought.

"Better," Stevens said. "Almost back to normal. I had worse in the war."

"So then it's not physical," van Norton said.

"Huh?" Stevens asked. "What's not physical?"

"Why you haven't resurfaced as Nucleus," van Norton said.

"Oh," Stevens said. "That." The two sat in silence for what seemed an interminably long time. "They almost killed me," Stevens said at last.

"But they didn't," van Norton observed. "Clearly."

"They tried to," Stevens said.

"Of course they tried to," van Norton said. "In less than a week, you made a huge dent in their operations. You think the mob is going to take that lying down? It's about power, and you're taking it away from them. Give up now, it won't make things any better. It might even make them worse. Here's the deal: they're *scared* of you."

"Wait," Stevens began, "I thought you said this was a crazy idea."

"And yet," van Norton countered, "I've been helping you out, every step of the way. Sometimes, just because something's crazy, it doesn't mean it's wrong."

"What are you saying?" Stevens asked.

"Finish what you started," van Norton said. "Fix what didn't work."

"How?" Stevens asked.

"Clearly," van Norton replied, "you need backup."

"Backup," Stevens said. *Could he be saying...?*

"You need some... *muscle,*" *van Norton said, grinning.* "*You might say that you need... a Strongman.*"

— § —

Friday, January 22, 1954

"I admit," Strongman said, looking himself over in his uniform, "I feel a bit ridiculous." While the cut and design of their outfits were nothing at all similar, Strongman's uniform used the same basic colors of blue and yellow as Nucleus, albeit inverted. Whereas Nucleus' uniform was predominantly yellow, with a blue cape, boots, gloves, trunks, and mask, Strongman's uniform featured a blue, sleeveless tunic and trunks, with yellow pants and a large, inverted yellow triangle across the front of his military-styled tunic; three buttons ran down each side of the triangle, and the high blue collar hung over the top side, making the triangle appear almost like a V. The boots were also blue, and the cape—held securely by red epaulets—was yellow. Strongman also wore a red belt with a single strap that ran diagonally across his chest from the epaulet on his left shoulder to a red satchel on his right hip. Like Nucleus, he also had a blue domino mask to conceal his identity.

"You look great," Nucleus said, appraising his friend. "Your tailor did a better job on your outfit than mine, I think."

"Hey, you *wanted* the traditional superhero look," Strongman countered playfully. The pair of friends walked out from the warmth of the main building of the van Norton estate, and into the frigid January air, and Nucleus was once again grateful that Strongman's tailor had used fabrics that, while lightweight and flexible, were also remarkably insulating. That he had learned to use his powers to subtly raise the temperature of the air around him certainly didn't hurt, either. Strongman's invulnerability also meant that temperature extremes didn't affect him as severely as a normal man, which was fortunate, as his uniform had no sleeves.

"So," Nucleus began, "how are we going to work this? You can't fly."

Strongman grinned. "Try to keep up." He crouched, and like a shot from a cannon, Strongman leaped into the air and soared away.

"Holy," Nucleus began, then rocketed into the air as well, pushing himself to keep up with his friend. Strongman bounded into the air over and over again. While he couldn't fly, he was still able to cover a remarkable distance in a short amount of time. Thanks to his super-strength, he could easily leap a half mile at a time. *If he really pushed himself,* Nucleus thought, *I wonder... just how far could he go?*

When Strongman finally stopped, he landed on a rooftop in a neighborhood known for its high crime rate. The glow from Nucleus' plasma added faintly to the illumination of the nearly-full moon as he landed on the rooftop next to his friend. They stood at the edge of the building, and peered over the side, toward the street below.

"I thought we'd start small tonight," Strongman said.

"What?" Nucleus asked, sarcastically. "We're not going to take on the mob directly on your first night out as a superhero?" The two friends shared a chuckle at that.

They scanned the streets of the neighborhood that sprawled out before them in silence for several minutes. "There," Strongman said at last, pointing. Nucleus followed the direction of his finger toward the street below, and saw a dark-skinned man in dark clothes standing near the wall of a building at the intersection of the street and an alleyway. The man appeared to be very agitated; he kept looking nervously around, and seemed unable to stand still in a way that couldn't be explained simply by the cold night air.

"Well," Nucleus said, grinning, "doesn't *he* look suspicious."

The pair of superheroes continued to watch the man in question, and it wasn't long before another person entered the scene: an older woman in a heavy coat and a thick, furry hat, a large purse slung over her shoulder and shopping bags in her hands. The man, attempting to act nonchalantly, warmed his hands with his breath while rubbing them together in front of his face, then shoved them back into his coat pockets as the woman walked past. Just after the woman passed him completely, he sprang into action, following her at a rapid pace. As he drew near, he began to pull his right hand out of his coat pocket, and Nucleus caught a glint of reflected light from an object he was holding in his hand.

"Go!" Nucleus hissed as the darkness of the night around him lit up with the illumination of the energetic plasma discharge of his powers launching him into the air. Strongman literally leaped into action, and by the time the dark-skinned man had finished pulling the pistol from his pocket, Nucleus had landed on the ground a few feet ahead of the woman, his fists glowing with energized plasma.

"Drop the gun, sir," Nucleus warned, then added, "Evening, ma'am." The woman dropped her grocery bags in shock at the sudden arrival of the yellow-and-blue-clad superhero, then spun to see the man behind her, the pistol in his hand half-raised in her direction. She yelped in terror. The man, eyes wide in shock at the immense misfortune of being caught in the act of an attempted mugging by the now-famous superhero Nucleus, pivoted to run...

Only to find himself staring at the chest of *another* superhero, a physically imposing brick wall of blue-and-yellow tights and cape stretched across a muscled mass of human being. With flight no longer being an option, the terrified man's brain switched to fight. He raised his pistol, pointing it directly at the chest of the man in front of him.

Strongman didn't even flinch. "I wouldn't do that, if I were you," he warned, gently. To no avail, it turned out, as an instant later, the world erupted in noise as the report of the pistol firing sounded. The deafening sound was nothing new to either superhero, nor apparently to the would-be mugger, as it failed to evoke any reaction from them as it instantly echoed off the brick walls of the buildings around them, assaulting their eardrums. The woman was not as accustomed to the sound of gunfire, however, and she screamed. Strongman looked down at his chest, and found the flattened bullet buried halfway through the material of the yellow triangle on the front of his tunic, directly between the pectoral muscles of his chest. He pulled the bullet, which now more closely resembled a dark metal mushroom than a projectile, from his clothing and held it up to inspect it.

"That was a brand new shirt," Strongman sighed, dropping the flattened projectile to the sidewalk. The would-be mugger's face went remarkably pale for a man with skin tone as dark as his. He froze in place, unable to move, the pistol still pointed at Strongman. The new hero reached out slowly, as unthreateningly as he could manage so as not to provoke the terrified man into unexpected action that could potentially hurt someone, and gently plucked the firearm, its barrel still releasing gentle wisps of smoke and condensed, steaming air, from his trembling grasp. Strongman glanced at the pistol appraisingly. "Colt .45 semiautomatic," he remarked. "Very nice." He shifted his grasp on the weapon, and pressed a button on the grip, causing the magazine to fall from the pistol to the pavement at his feet. He then tugged firmly on the slide at the top of the pistol, and an unfired round flew from chamber, where it, too, clattered to the concrete of the sidewalk where they stood. The ammunition now safely removed from the weapon, Strongman tossed it aside, where it clattered to the ground a satisfyingly safe distance from the magazine and now-de-chambered round. "We won't be needing that anymore," Strongman added with a gentle grin. He reached out once more and firmly grasped the would-be mugger's shoulder; he wouldn't be going anywhere until Strongman decided otherwise. Strongman spun the man around until he faced the woman, who was still shaking in terror. "I believe you owe this woman an apology."

"I-I-I," the man began to stammmer, his voice barely above a whisper.

"You'll have to speak up, sir," Nucleus interjected, smiling broadly, "it's very hard to hear you."

"I-I'm sorry," the man said, almost imperceptibly louder.

"What was that?" Strongman asked. He grabbed the man with both hands on either shoulder, squeezed slightly, and lifted the man nearly a full inch off of the ground. "You'll have to be more specific."

"I'm sorry," the man repeated, his voice becoming louder with each repetition, until he was shouting. "I'm sorry! I'm sorry! *I'm sorry!*" He was on the verge of tears now in his terror, and Strongman put him back down on the sidewalk.

Nucleus looked up and saw that faces were beginning to emerge in the windows of the buildings in the neighborhood. Some windows opened, and curious heads stuck out to see what all the commotion was about.

"In case no one has done so already," Nucleus announced loudly to the growing assembly of onlookers, "I'd recommend that someone call the police to come pick this man up." A few heads disappeared, presumably heading inside to find their telephones and make those calls. Nucleus turned his attention back to the woman. She looked to be in her fifties or sixties, and the blood had drained from her face, leaving her very pale. "It's all right now, ma'am," Nucleus said reassuringly.

— § —

"Gentlemen," Nucleus announced as the police cruiser arrived and two police officers stepped out into the frigid night air. They were clad in the New York Police Department's winter uniform, with dark, heavy overcoats and hats, both adorned with shining police badges. "I'd like to introduce you to a friend of mine: Strongman." The officers looked at the new hero, obviously failing to hide a slight unease.

"It's a pleasure, officers," Strongman said warmly. He noticed that they were staring at the ragged bullet hole in the center of his chest. "Yes, that." He indicated the would-be mugger, who was sitting uncomfortably on the cold concrete of the sidewalk, his hands bound together in front of him as he leaned against the equally cold brick of the nearest building, with a wave of his hand. "We caught this man trying to rob this woman," he waved his hand again, to indicate the older woman, who was standing with Nucleus a few feet away. "When we intervened, he shot me." Their eyes widened. "I'm all right," he assured them. "I'm not just strong, thankfully. I wish I could say the same for my shirt. Anyhow, I disarmed him. The weapon is over there," he indicated the pistol, still where he'd thrown it earlier, "and the ammunition is here," he indicated the ground at his feet.

The officers looked at Nucleus and the woman. "It's true, officers," she said, before they could ask. "These two young men saved my life."

One of the officers pulled out a notebook. Introducing himself as Officer Phillips, he took the statements of the heroes and the woman while his partner, who introduced himself as Officer Davis, placed the would-be mugger in handcuffs, then moved him into the back of the patrol car. Once the officers collected the pistol and ammunition, they climbed back into their patrol car and drove off. Nucleus turned to the woman, who had told the police that her name was Claire McGannon.

"Do you need someone to walk you the rest of the way home?" Nucleus asked Claire.

"If it's not too much trouble," Claire said. "I *would feel much better.*"

"It's not a problem at all, ma'am," Nucleus replied. Each taking one of the bags of groceries that Claire had dropped when the robbery began, Nucleus and Strongman walked on either side of her as she led them to the apartment building that she called home. Thanking them for their help, Claire went inside, leaving the two heroes alone on the sidewalk.

"That," Strongman began, searching for the right words. "That felt pretty good."

"That it did," Nucleus agreed. "Let's keep moving." He launched himself into the air, and Strongman leaped to follow his friend.

CHAPTER NINE

Erich Eidelmann surveyed the men lined up in a military formation before him. They stood, silent and rigidly still, in neat rows as he paced methodically in front of them, his hands clasped behind his back. Three men followed closely behind him.

"Excellent," he observed to one of the men closest to him. "Do you believe that they are ready?" he asked, indicating the assembled men with the inclination of his head.

The man nearest to Eidelmann hesitated, glancing to the other two men, but he found no reassurance in their eyes. Nevertheless, they feared Eidelmann, having seen his power firsthand. They did not want to disappoint the *übermensch* in their presence. They knew what could happen to anyone unfortunate enough to do so.

"I," the man began slowly, "believe so, *mein Herr.*"

Eidelmann stopped abruptly. He turned, slowly and menacingly; he had caught the hesitation and prevarication in the man's response. "Do not lie to me," he said, his voice low and dangerous. "You have had months to prepare."

"*Mein Herr,*" the man began, unable to completely hide the fear creeping into his voice, "we do not know what to expect. Certainly, there will be police presence when we arrive, but there is now news of another *übermensch* like yourself..."

"I will deal with him," Eidelmann replied harshly, cutting the other man off. "Are you afraid of a few policemen? We have an *army*."

"Our men will have no trouble with policemen," the man replied confidently.

"Then we are ready," Eidelmann said. It was clear that he would brook no opposition. The men gaped for a moment, then the man that Eidelmann had been speaking with came to attention, snapped his heels together, and bowed slightly from the waist.

"*Jawohl, mein Herr,*" he said, barely hiding the uncertainty in his voice. Having heard what he wanted to hear, Eidelmann smiled wickedly. He nodded to the men and abruptly turned. Within moments, he had stalked briskly away, back toward the village that the enclave of Nazi expatriates had come to call home. The men looked to one another, uncertainty plain on their faces. After a moment, they turned to face the formation of men before them.

"Dismissed," the man who had been speaking to Eidelmann ordered loudly. The formation quickly split up, and the men that had been standing rigidly still moments earlier dispersed. "Madness," he muttered softly. His companions nodded their agreement, and they shared worried glances as they watched the formation disperse.

As that proceeded, Eidelmann marched toward the central camp of the Nazi village. The area was home to several small buildings. Most were homes, with a handful of modest shops, and they formed an orderly ring around a well-maintained grassy park. One end was open to the path that Eidelmann walked upon as he entered the village. Directly opposite the path, on the other side of the small park, was a building that had come to house the administration of the Nazi enclave.

Eidelmann strode through the park, at the center of which stood a flagpole that defiantly flew the flag of the Third Reich. Here, at least, the Reich remained. Here, this community sought to bring about the Reich's return, like a phoenix from the ashes of defeat.

Passing the flagpole, Eidelmann continued forward, and entered the small administration building. He passed the secretary seated at the modest desk within the main entry, and she started to rise to stop his unannounced visit, but she was too slow, and he burst into the office beyond. Schmachenberg, the leader of the Nazi enclave, looked up from the papers on his desk at the unexpected intrusion. His eyes immediately narrowed in anger and annoyance at the interruption.

"*Herr Eidelmann,*" Schmachenberg began, unable to conceal the irritation in his tone.

"We are leaving," Eidelmann interrupted, cutting off any rebuke Schmachenberg had before it could be delivered.

Schmachenberg sat in dumbfounded silence, blinking in surprise at the insolence on display before him. After a moment, he found his voice. "We?" he asked. "Your little militia takes its orders from *me*. They are going nowhere, least of all with you. If you want to get yourself killed on a foolhardy assault on the American capitol, be my guest, but you will do so alone."

"They follow *me*, old man," Eidelmann said with a wicked smile. "Your way lost the war. Your way will have us sit for generations doing nothing to restore the Reich! Your way has failed! We. Are. Leaving."

"You will die," Schmachenberg said flatly. "As will any fool who follows you." He sighed, then waved a dismissive hand at Eidelmann. "Go. Die. It will do us all a favor to be rid of you."

Eidelmann narrowed his eyes, biting back the retort that begged to be loosed from his lips. He turned and left, not bothering to bestow any courtesies upon Schmachenberg.

— § —

Eidelmann had spent years preparing for this moment. Schmachenberg was such a myopic fool, he hadn't realized the extent of the planning and preparation that Eidelmann had undertaken to get to this point. He had secretly amassed a small fortune, through means both legitimate and otherwise, and had equipped his forces with weaponry and a small cargo vessel.

The ship had served several purposes: it had brought in a not-insignificant flow of currency through both legitimate shipping and smuggling; it had established itself as a known entity in American shipping lanes, which would help alleviate suspicion later on; and the contacts it had opened up through smuggling operations had enabled Eidelmann to acquire the weapons he'd needed to equip his men.

Evening was beginning to give way to night as his men, posing as laborers and passengers, loaded themselves and their crates of equipment and supplies aboard the small freighter. The last vestiges of sunlight disappeared beneath the horizon as the ship's crew—also loyal followers—drew up the gangplank and the ship pushed away from the dock.

The voyage, Eidelmann knew, would take a month. The ship would travel north along the eastern coast of South America, making stops along the way for trading and resupply. Once they reached the northern shores of Brazil, they would set out into the open seas, stopping briefly at ports in the Caribbean as they continued north toward the United States. After reaching Florida, they would again hug the coastline, which would provide a measure of safety from the conditions that could be found far out into the oceans, which a freighter like theirs would be ill-equipped to handle.

It would be a long journey, but they would ultimately reach their destination: New York City, the economic and cultural hub of the United States. Less heavily defended than the country's capitol in Washington, D.C., it would make for an excellent target for their first strike to restore the Reich. They would subjugate the city, recruit allies, and expand from there. It would take time, yes, but it was nowhere near the snail's pace of Schmachenberg's technology-dependent plotting.

At each of their stops, Eidelmann made sure to get the latest news out of New York. The emergence of the man who had taken to calling himself Nucleus just before Christmas had been concerning, but then he had disappeared. As the ship reached Florida, however, the relief at that news had not only been dashed by word of Nucleus' return, it had been annihilated at the revelation of a second costumed *übermensch*, this one taking the sobriquet of Strongman. Eidelmann remained assured that he could dispatch both men—he had the powers of a god, after all.

In fact, he had become more convinced during the voyage that, perhaps, he should take on a sobriquet of his own, and he had the perfect name in mind. His powers gave him control over lightning, just like the ancient Norse god of thunder. He would take on the name of that god— the proper *German* name of that god. He would be *Donner*.

No, he decided, he *was* Donner.

Chapter Ten

Monday, February 1, 1954

Alex Stevens looked up from the bench where he sat in Central Park as his friend, Percy van Norton, walked toward him. "Percy," he greeted warmly. "How are you?"

Van Norton smiled at his friend, who rose to shake his hand. "Good," he replied. "You?"

"Good," Stevens said as well, sitting back down on the bench. As van Norton took a seat beside him, Stevens asked, "What did you want to see me about?"

Van Norton's head turned quickly to look at his friend in confusion. "Me?" he asked. "I thought *you wanted to see me.*"

Before Stevens could add his own confused reply, a voice came from behind them, "Actually, *I'm* the one who wanted to see both of you." The two jumped to their feet, spinning to face the unexpected arrival, their stances in trained fighting positions, ready for combat. They found another man in a dark business suit and matching trench coat standing about ten feet behind the bench, his arms crossed, a dark fedora perched atop his head. They began to relax, albeit slightly, as they recognized the man.

"Higgins?" Stevens asked. "Is that you?"

"Jesus," van Norton muttered. "It's the Shield."

Joe Higgins chuckled at the name. "Yeah, it's me, guys." His arms dropped to his sides and he began to walk toward the bench. "It's been a while."

"What brings you out here to New York?" Stevens asked as Higgins reached them.

Higgins tilted his head and looked at him from the corner of his eyes, a lopsided grin crossing his pursed lips. "Really?" he asked. "Two new superheroes emerge in your hometown, with code names and powers identical to yours…"

"Incredible coincidence," van Norton deadpanned, "isn't it?"

"We're not idiots," Higgins replied.

"'We?'" Stevens asked.

Higgins reached into his jacket pocket and pulled out his wallet. He flipped it open, revealing a shining badge and an identification card. "Special Agent Joe Higgins, FBI," Higgins said by way of introduction.

"You'll always be the Shield to me," van Norton quipped.

"Nice," Higgins replied sarcastically. "We know exactly who you are, so it's obvious you're not trying to hide from us."

"Why should we need to hide from the government?" Stevens asked. "We're just trying to help."

"What you're doing," Higgins said, "is acting as vigilantes. Strictly speaking, you're breaking the law." He paused for a moment, then continued, "But you've been doing some good, and you're not getting out of hand about it, so we've been willing to look the other way, for now."

"So, what you're saying," van Norton said seriously, "is that you're here as a warning to not let things get too out of hand, and you're the friendly face that also happens to know who we really are."

"Nail on the head," Higgins confirmed. "Look, don't get me wrong. You *are* doing some good here. You've actually made a dent in some of the organized crime here in New York. Just remember, we're watching, so don't let things get out of hand."

"And by 'out of hand,'" Stevens began, "you mean…"

"I mean," Higgins clarified, "you've done a good job by working with the police, but don't forget that you're still private citizens. Your ability to... *intervene* in law enforcement is limited."

Stevens nodded. "I've never forgotten that," he said.

"Make sure that you don't," Higgins said. He sighed. "We're entering some uncharted waters here. There's been some rumblings on the Hill about you two."

"You mean," van Norton began.

Higgins nodded. "McCarthy," he confirmed. "The man is paranoid, and thinks everyone is secretly a communist. Conveniently, his political rivals are usually at the top of his list, and you don't rate that in his eyes, yet. Just..." he paused, clearly looking to phrase his next words carefully, "just watch your six, guys. *I* know you two aren't Reds, but hardly anyone knows who's really under the masks."

— $ —

"Maybe Higgins is right," van Norton said as he and Stevens sat together in the study—Stevens had finally asked what the room with all the bookshelves was—later that evening.

"About what?" Stevens asked.

"About the masks," van Norton said. "Maybe people will trust us more if they have a real name to go with the hero."

"No way," Stevens said. "I'm not putting my family at risk of a mob hit."

"I hadn't thought of that," van Norton admitted. "My family has always had security for that kind of thing. Sometimes I forget that you don't have things like that."

Stevens rolled his eyes. "You really did grow up in a different world," he said.

"I'm learning," van Norton replied. "Well, maybe you don't have to do it. But maybe it would help if one of us did."

"You're serious," Stevens observed.

"Yes," van Norton replied. "I already told my parents about my powers after we got back from the war. They weren't thrilled about me using my accounts to pay for all of this, but it's my money."

"I'd take some time to think about it," Stevens cautioned. "That's the kind of thing that you can't take back."

Van Norton nodded. "You're right," he admitted. "I just want to help."

— § —

John Sterling cradled the lifeless body of his father in his arms. He had come home this evening, only to find his father face down in a pool of his own blood, laying in front of the fireplace, on the floor of the main room of the family estate. He remembered seeing a car leaving the grounds as he came home. They couldn't be far, he realized. He'd only been home a few minutes. His vision literally went red. He'd always thought that was just an expression, but the rage he was feeling was simply that palpable.

Sterling gently lowered his father's body back to the carpet, irretrievably stained with his pooled blood. He bowed his head, paying his father a moment of silent prayer. Rising to his feet, Sterling clenched his fists, and strode out of the room. His pace quickened as he advanced, and by the time he left the front doors of the mansion, he was moving at a brisk run. He knew that he would never catch the murderers' car at this speed... but he also knew that he was capable of moving *much* faster. He pushed himself up, the immense strength gathered in his muscles causing him to leap incredibly high into the air, but before he reached the top of the arc, another sensation that he was still learning to trust and control kicked in. He reached the top of the arc from his leap... and kept going. Sterling scanned the road below him as he soared over the treetops.

It didn't take long before he spotted the headlights. There was only a single car on the road. It *had* to be them. Sterling let himself begin to drop, angling his descent toward the car. Within moments, he landed on the roof of the car with a dull thump. Using another sense that he was still developing, he magnetized himself to the car, preventing himself from simply sliding off the smooth surface.

"What was that?" a voice said from inside the car.

"I dunno," another voice replied. "Take a look." A moment later, a head peeked up from the front passenger side window. Eyes wide in shock, it disappeared just as quickly.

"Jesus!" the first voice shouted. "There's a guy on the roof!"

"Well, get 'im off!" the second voice shouted back.

After a moment, Sterling heard a raspy mechanical sound: someone was racking the chamber of a rifle of some sort. Almost as soon as the thought registered, he was greeted by a hail of bullets that tore through the roof around the hand that he had magnetized to the car. His head snapped back as one punched into his jaw like a fist. Fortunately for Sterling, the bullet was not nearly enough to penetrate his nigh-invulnerable hide. He flexed the muscles in his jaw, working out the kink he'd developed from the blow he'd just taken.

The roof of the car was shredded, filled with holes like a piece of Swiss cheese. With his free hand, Sterling forced his fingers through a group of holes. He made a fist, then with a shriek of tearing metal, he ripped a chunk of the roof away. Releasing his grip, he flung the metal into the air behind him, and it bounced off of the pavement, receding far into the distance as the car sped through the lonely road. He then reached into the car and grabbed the shirt of the man in the passenger seat, who was holding a Thompson submachine gun and wearing an expression that combined shock and terror. Sterling hefted the man effortlessly out of his seat.

"Who are you?" he bellowed into the man's terrified face. "Why did you kill my father?" Instead of answering, the man fainted. As he dropped the unconscious man back into the seat, he noticed the growing, wet stain on the front of his pants. Sterling turned his attention to the man in the driver's seat. "Stop the car!" he ordered. Wisely, the driver complied. As the car rolled to a stop on the side of the road, Sterling jumped off of the roof and ripped the driver's door from its hinges. Sterling grabbed the man inside and pulled him out, holding him up by the front of his shirt. The man's feet dangled more than two feet in the air.

"He shouldn't'a said no," the driver spat back, defiantly. Sterling's arm quavered in rage and he lifted the driver slightly higher. Sterling's eyes narrowed dangerously. "The boss gave him a chance to play ball."

"Who," Sterling forced through gritted teeth, "is the 'boss?'"

"Who's the boss?" the driver practically laughed. "Are you stupid, kid? Everybody knows Johnny Barone." Sterling indeed recognized the name: Johnny Barone was the up-and-coming young head of one of the Italian mafia families, who had taken over after his own father had died under "mysterious" circumstances a year earlier.

Sterling was confused. "Why would Johnny Barone have my dad killed?"

"We wasn't gonna kill him," the driver said. "We was just gonna have a talk with him, but then he pulled out a gun. It was self-defense."

"You lying son of a bitch," Sterling retorted, pulling the driver's face to his. "There was no gun in the room with my father's body, and you were in *his* home. You were trying to extort him!"

"Your word against mine, kid," the driver said, "and you wasn't there."

Sterling wanted to smash the man's smug face in with his bare hands. He could do it, easily. But he knew that's not what his father would have wanted. If he killed this man, he'd be no better than he was. There were laws for a reason. He had to let the police and the courts do their job. Still clutching the man, who was showing remarkably little fear for someone in his situation, by the front of his shirt, Sterling grabbed the door that he'd torn from the car and wrapped it around the driver like it was tin foil.

Once the man was suitably restrained, he dropped him to the ground with a satisfying clang of metal on pavement, then turned back to the car. The passenger was nowhere to be found. *He must have woken up while I was busy with his buddy*, Sterling thought. He looked up and down the road, but couldn't see the other man anywhere. *He must have run into the woods*, Sterling thought. *There's no way I'll find him when it's this dark out.*

Sterling turned back to the man he'd captured. He grabbed the man under one arm and leaped into the sky.

— § —

John Sterling watched in appreciation as the painter finished his work on the frosted glass of the office door. He'd leased a modest office near downtown Manhattan, and had moved in a desk, a few chairs, and a sofa so far, and he was reclining in his chair behind the desk, his fingers steepled before his face. He'd been reading a newspaper, but it sat, forgotten, on his desk. While the police had arrested the man that he'd caught fleeing the scene of his father's murder, within hours he'd been released on bond, and the general consensus was that none of the charges would stick. Sickened and frustrated, Sterling had spent days trying to figure out what he could do about it.

In the end, despite the whispered comments from the police officers who had taken his statement and thought that he couldn't hear them talking, he was *not* going to be a superhero like Nucleus or Strongman. Their activities struck him as far too close to the line of vigilantism for his comfort. No, if he couldn't do anything about his father's murder right now, he'd let the police do their work and focus on things that he could do something about. He was, therefore, opening up shop as a private investigator, albeit with a nod to the growing trend of heroes: he was going to operate under the name Steel Sterling. While not a secret identity, the nom de plume managed to hint at his extraordinary abilities. He was fully licensed, bonded, and now he had a literal place to hang his hat: there was a coat rack in the corner near the door.

He had already taken on his first case, and it was a bizarre one. Following the trail of a series of bank robberies had led him to an actual castle that someone had built more than a hundred miles outside of the city, guarded with archers, machine guns, and hidden trap doors run by a man in a garish medieval knight costume that called himself the Black Knight. In the end, the castle was destroyed when a magazine of explosives detonated, presumably taking the Black Knight with it. Then the Black Knight resurfaced two days ago, attempting to recruit new flunkies by breaking them out of jail. Sterling's thoughts were interrupted by a knock at the door. Looking up, he spotted a pair of men in bright, blue-and-yellow costumes, complete with capes, standing in the open doorway. The painter was packing up his brushes and supplies, and had just placed a sign that read "Wet Paint" on the glass under the newly-finished sign, which read, "Steel Sterling, Private Investigator."

"Nucleus," Sterling said in recognition. "Strongman. I should have guessed that it would just be a matter of time before you paid me a visit." He rose from his seat, stepped out in front of his desk, and extended his right hand in greeting. "John Sterling," he said, introducing himself. Sterling shook hands with the heroes, then asked, "What brings you here?"

Nucleus and Strongman glanced at one another. "We heard about you in the papers," Nucleus began, then added, "My condolences about your father." Sterling nodded in appreciation for their consideration, and Nucleus continued, "We weren't quite sure what to make of you. You've set yourself up as a private eye, but... well, it sounded more like you're acting like a superhero."

"I'm no vigilante," Sterling insisted. "Things got... well, things got *weird* on the Black Knight case, but I'm no superhero. I'm just a private investigator who happens to have super powers."

"About that," Strongman interjected. "Has there been any... blow-back from that? Being public with your identity?"

"I am who and what I am," Sterling replied. "People can accept me for that, or not. I'm operating within the law, and there's nothing illegal about being a licensed private investigator." He arched an eyebrow. "Are you considering a career change?"

"Not exactly," Strongman replied. He indicated Nucleus, "My colleague and I are concerned about the repercussions to our families if one of us were to go public with his identity, especially given the, ah, bad blood between us and the mob these days."

"Understandable," Sterling said. "My father was my only living relative. That's... not exactly a concern for me now."

"That's not why we came," Nucleus interrupted. "We wanted to meet you, to get a feel for you. Like you said, though, you're not a superhero, but you do have powers. If we ever needed your help with something... would you be willing to help us?"

"My fee is one hundred dollars a day, plus expenses," Sterling replied, then added, "And don't even think of asking me to do something illegal or to put on a costume."

"Never," Nucleus said immediately.

"Unless you gentlemen have some work for me," Sterling said, extending his hand once more, "it was a pleasure meeting you."

They exchanged goodbyes, shook hands once again, and the two heroes left. Sterling went back to reading his newspaper, and after a few minutes, there was another knock at the door.

"Something else I can do for you, gentlemen?" he asked without looking up.

A woman's voice replied, "Excuse me?" Sterling's head shot up, and he quickly rose from his seat.

"Sorry, miss," he said. "I thought you were someone else." He stepped over to her from behind his desk and extended his hand in greeting. "John Sterling."

"Dora Cummings," she said, taking his hand.

"How can I help you, Miss Cummings?" Sterling asked, waving a hand to indicate the seats in front of his desk.

"My father has been kidnapped," she said, taking the seat that Sterling offered to her, "by someone calling himself Dr. Yar. Here, I found this note when I got home."

Taking the note, Sterling asked, "Why not go to the police? They're better suited to finding a kidnapper."

"Read the note," Dora urged. "He'll kill my father *and me! I couldn't go to the police. You're my only hope!*"

Sterling read the note, then rubbed his chin thoughtfully. "I take it that your father is Dr. Walter Cummings?" Dr. Cummings was a famed scientist and industrialist.

"Yes," Dora confirmed.

"Okay," Sterling said. "I'll take your case." He laid out his fees, and the pair began working to figure out where Dora's father had been taken.

Chapter Eleven

The man ran down the alleyway, turning as he ran to look behind him. An indistinct form moved in the shadows of the alley behind him, leaping silently from object to object, keeping pace with the running man.

His attention on the form that was pursuing him, rather than what was in front of him, the running man collided with a pair of steel trash cans. They clattered loudly as they fell to the pavement, and the man stumbled to the ground. As he fell, he reached for his waist with one hand, his other hand stretched out to break his fall.

The man spun to his back as he hit the ground, and he faced the direction from which he had come. As he turned, he pulled a pistol from his waistline under his heavy winter coat. He took aim, his arm trembling slightly. Whoever or *whatever* had been chasing him mere moments before was now completely still, concealed in the heavy shadows of the alleyway at night.

For several moments, the man sat in silence, desperately looking for a target. None presented themselves until a soft skittering sound emerged from the shadows. He opened fire, and the alley was consumed in three loud thunderclaps and flashes of light. The casings from his expended ammunition clinked as they rolled into each other, steaming, on the freezing pavement to his right. A rat scurried away, illuminated briefly as it fled.

Light glinted quickly as something shot out from the shadows. Before the man could bring his gun to bear, the object struck his hand. He lost his grip on the pistol as pain erupted across the back of his hand. The gun clattered to the ground, and as he instinctively reached for his injury with his other, uninjured hand, a much larger, darker shape rocketed toward him from the shadows.

The shape slammed into the man, and they rolled together for a moment. The shape resolved into a man wearing a black leather outfit. A hood flared out around his head like the neck of a cobra, and stylized fangs framed the mask that concealed the top half of the face of the man in the black costume. He cocked an arm back, and slammed a fist into the face of the now-disarmed man he'd been chasing.

"Where are you keeping the girl?" the man in black demanded. His voice was gravelly and laced with menace.

"Who *are* you?" the disarmed man asked in shock.

The man in black grabbed the other man roughly by his collar and pulled him so their faces were just inches apart. "I'm the Black Cobra," he hissed. "And you haven't answered my question."

"I don't know *nothin'*," the man muttered defiantly.

The Black Cobra let go of the man with his right hand, while maintaining his grasp on the man's collar with his left. He backhanded the man across the jaw with his now-free right hand, the black leather of his glove making a smacking sound upon impact with the man's face.

"Don't lie to me," the Black Cobra said icily. "Where is the girl?" He looked up as sirens began to wail in the distance and slowly grew nearer. He looked back at the man in his grasp. "Last chance."

The man grinned, his teeth stained red with blood. "What girl?"

The Black Cobra drew back his fist and punched the man in the face. The man's nose bent at an unnatural angle and blood began to flow from his nostrils. The sirens grew louder, and the Black Cobra dropped the man to the ground.

A police cruiser screeched to a halt at the mouth of the alley. The Black Cobra leaped away from the man, somersaulting into the darkened alley. The police officer barely had time to register that the black-clad man had even been there as he jumped out of his car, drawing his sidearm. He aimed his service revolver down the alleyway, bewildered.

—§—

Jim Hornsby closed the front door of his family's home quietly as he entered. A fair-skinned, light-haired young man, he was powerfully built, but his loose-fitting business suit concealed that fact from most people's notice. He gently turned the latch, locking the deadbolt, and straightened his posture.

"And just where have you been?" a stern man's voice rang out from behind Jim. "It's late, and we have work in the morning." Jim forced himself to relax, then turned. His father stood in the hallway, arms crossed over a robe and pajamas.

"I went to a movie," Jim said. "I'll be fine for work in the morning, dad." Jim made his way toward the stairs, but his father blocked his path.

"You need to stop wasting your time on trivialities," Jim's father declared. "If you're going to make it through law school, you need to focus on what matters. Bad enough you lost so much time going to Korea." Jim sighed. His father was the district attorney, and expected with absolute certainty that Jim and his younger brother, Bob, would follow in his footsteps and become attorneys as well.

Jim, however, had no desire to become an attorney. His father had pressed him into a job as a clerk in the district attorney's office, a position which he'd grudgingly accepted. Jim had told his father on several occasions that he had no desire to enter the law, but his father refused to listen. "Dad," Jim began, "we've talked about this…"

"Pish posh," his father interrupted dismissively. "Of course you want to be an attorney. No one wants to be a *clerk forever.*"

"I don't," Jim began.

"None of that," his father scolded mildly. "All that time in the army just has you confused. We've had this plan for years."

You've *had this plan,* Jim thought bitterly. *And I was in the Marines.* Knowing this would go nowhere, he said instead, "Look, dad, I'm tired and I'd like to go to bed. I'll see you in the morning, all right?"

Jim's father smiled and stepped aside. "All right, son," he said. "Good night."

"Good night, dad," Jim replied, and made his way up the stairs. He went down the hallway and reached out to open the door to his room.

Before he turned the knob, he paused. He could hear noises coming from inside, and there was a cold draft coming from under the door. His eyes narrowed, and his muscles tensed. Turning the knob quickly, he threw the door open and assumed a fighting stance.

His window was open, and his brother Bob was crouched near it, going through a duffel bag on the floor below the window.

"What the hell are you doing?" Jim demanded, relaxing his posture back to normal. Bob didn't reply. A senior in high school, Bob had dark hair like their father, and was in excellent shape from years of school athletics programs. He pulled a black leather garment from the bag. It had a large, cowled hood that featured stylized fangs on either side of a half-mask.

"Found this outside on the roof next to your window," Bob said, holding the garment up for display. "I heard someone walking on the roof, and when I checked, there it was."

Great, Jim thought. "And you just brought it inside?" he asked. "It could have been something dangerous. Dad's the D.A.; a lot of bad people would want to hurt him."

Bob was quiet for a moment. "I hadn't thought of that," he admitted. He looked back at his older brother. "Still, what is this? I don't think it's a coincidence that it showed up right when you got home. If I didn't know better, I'd say it looks like that Black Cobra I've read about in the papers."

Jim closed the door to his bedroom. "Shut the window," he said. "It's cold outside." Bob rose and shut the window as he'd been told. When he was finished turning the latch, Jim waved a hand toward the bed and said, "Sit down."

Bob sat on the edge of the bed, and Jim spun the wooden chair from under the desk along the wall next to the bed, sitting backwards on the chair and resting his arms on the chair's back as he leaned forward. He took a deep breath, held it for a moment, then exhaled slowly. Bob looked at him expectantly.

"I'm the Black Cobra," Jim confessed. Bob didn't seem overly surprised; he'd already deduced as much after finding the costume.

"Do you have powers?" Bob asked.

"No," Jim answered. "I learned how to fight in the war, and I learned martial arts when I was in Korea. *Tae Kwon Do, Kuk Sool Won,* that sort of thing." Bob's eyes glazed over at the unfamiliar names of the Korean martial arts. "I never knew what I wanted to do with my life," Jim continued, "until I got home from Korea. Dad wants us to go into the law, but the law doesn't always work. I want to be there to help the people the law is failing. To do the things that the law can't."

Bob shifted uncomfortably on the bed. "Are," he began, "are you killing people?"

"No," Jim replied adamantly. "I don't mind the bad guys thinking that I do, or that I might, but I'm not killing people. The law isn't perfect, but I'm not judge, jury, and executioner. I'm out there to stop people from getting hurt, and to help the police get evidence they couldn't get otherwise. Not to kill."

"Okay," Bob said, relaxing. He paused a moment, then said, "I want in."

Jim sat up straight. "No way," he said. "It's too dangerous. You're just a kid."

"I'm turning eighteen next month," Bob shot back. "The same age as you when you went to Korea."

"This is different," Jim said.

"We're in the same boat," Bob countered. "I don't want what dad's pushing on us any more than you do. I *do* want this. I have for a while now." Jim sighed, but before he could argue the point, Bob continued, "I was already planning something like this. I'm doing this, with or without your help."

"I'll be damned if I let you get yourself killed," Jim said, resigned. "All right. I'll train you, but you don't go out into the field until I say you're ready."

— § —

Nucleus and Strongman stood at the edge of the roof of an apartment building that overlooked a battered-looking neighborhood. Night had descended upon the city hours earlier, and it had proven to be a quiet night so far. The white noise of the city filled the air: the soft drone of traffic, the breeze blowing between the buildings, and the rustling of leaves in the trees that lined the sidewalks. The two men scanned the area as their breath puffed into clouds of steam in the cold winter night.

For the past couple of weeks, the news had been reporting sightings of a masked vigilante who called himself the Black Cobra and had been stalking criminals in this part of the city. The Black Cobra remained very much a mystery: there were no photos of him, and descriptions ranged from the mundane—he wore all black leather—to the fantastic—he transformed into an actual, giant cobra. His motives remained a mystery.

The pressure that Nucleus and Strongman were feeling from Washington pushed them to proactively seek out those new heroes that were beginning to emerge. They had already met with Steel Sterling, who still insisted that he was most definitely *not* a superhero, despite the outlandish situations his cases as a private investigator had repeatedly landed him in. He, at least, had been easy to find, before he left for Brazil a few days after their conversation with him. The Black Cobra, however, remained elusive. Nucleus and Strongman had staked out this neighborhood for the last three days. Unsure what exactly it was that they were looking for, they waited, hoping perhaps to catch him in action.

"You seem to be looking for someone," a rough voice emerged from the shadows behind Nucleus and Strongman. They spun in surprise, assuming fighting postures. The air around Nucleus' fists began to glow and crackle with energized plasma. A figure emerged from the shadows, clad in black from head to toe. His hood flared out around his head like a cobra. "Relax, gentlemen," the Black Cobra said. "If I intended you harm, you would not have even known I was here first." He spread his hands at his sides. "I come in peace."

Nucleus and Strongman relaxed somewhat. They straightened their postures and Nucleus extinguished his plasma, but they remained wary.

"You're the Black Cobra, I take it," Nucleus said, looking pointedly at the cowl.

"Yes," the Black Cobra said. "Nucleus and Strongman. Come to make sure I'm not a psychotic killer, I take it?"

"Something like that," Nucleus acknowledged. He hesitated, then asked, "Are you?"

The Black Cobra laughed heartily for a moment, then said, "No. I'm no killer. I run around in this, though," he indicated his costume, "so I guess the jury's still out on the other bit."

"For all of us," Strongman interjected, eliciting a chuckle from all three of the heroes. "In all seriousness," Strongman continued after a moment, "we needed to get a read on you. There have been a lot of stories going around."

"I understand," the Black Cobra said. "Some misinformation is useful to how I operate."

"We also wanted to make you aware," Nucleus continued, "that there's been some rumblings in Washington about all of the superheroes popping up."

"McCarthy," the Black Cobra said.

"Exactly," Nucleus acknowldeged. "They were already taking a look at comic books, after that book came out by that psychiatrist, Wertham. Now there's real-life superheroes running around. As long as we don't cross the line, they're willing to look the other way. For now, at least."

The Black Cobra nodded thoughtfully. He hadn't considered the broader implications of his costumed identity. He'd wanted to help the people that slipped through the cracks of the law. Now, he was facing a much bigger, faceless threat. He squared his shoulders. "I see," he said, after a moment.

Chapter Twelve

Monday, February 8, 1954

Strongman stepped up to the podium at the steps of city hall. Dozens of reporters stood facing the dais, as well as a crowd of several hundred spectators. Nucleus stood just behind his friend, offering his silent support.

Flash bulbs exploded as photographers jockeyed for position, and television news cameras stood ready, waiting. The murmur of voices quieted as Strongman placed his hands on the podium, then looked up to address the crowd. This was the first press conference ever given by a superhero. This was *history*, and everyone knew it.

"Ladies and gentlemen," Strongman began, "thank you for coming. Sorry it's so cold today." The crowd chuckled. "For the past couple weeks, you've come to know me, and what I stand for. But there are some who ask who it is behind the masks, and how we can be trusted." A murmur went through the crowd. "I should hope that my actions have put some of those fears to rest. But there is also an understandable fear there, a fear of the unknown. But the unknown is just something temporarily hidden, temporarily not understood." He paused, letting his words sink in.

"My friend, Nucleus," Strongman said, indicating the other hero standing behind him with a wave of his hand, "wears his mask to protect the people he loves. His concern is justifiable; the forces that we face have little compunction to refrain from harming those closest to us if they cannot harm us directly." Murmurs and nods went through the crowd.

"There has been some question," Strongman continued, "regarding the patriotism of masked heroes like Nucleus and myself. I ask, would anyone *but* a patriot risk his life to protect his community or his nation?" More murmurs and nods of assent rippled through the gathered crowd.

"I wore this mask," Strongman said, "because Nucleus did. He was the first hero. He set the standard. For him, the mask makes sense, but I didn't examine my own reasons. Not at first." Strongman reached up with both hands, touching either side of his mask. A gasp went through the crowd, and the air filled with the sound of cameras clicking in time with a flurry of exploding flashbulbs. He peeled the mask away from his eyes, exposing his face for the world to see. "My name is Percy van Norton," he said. "I am Strongman."

Strongman took a half-step back from the podium as the assembled reporters surged forward, all yelling questions. He closed his eyes for a moment, and took a deep breath. He held it for a second, then exhaled slowly. He opened his eyes again, and looked at the crowd of reporters clamoring for his attention.

"Yes," Strongman said, pointing to one of the reporters. The man was of average height and build, and wore an insulated black trench coat over a gray suit, with a matching gray fedora and a black scarf as a concession to the cold. Even then, the coat was left open. The reporter held a narrow notebook in his hand, and already had nearly filled a page with hastily-scrawled notes.

"Kent Schreiber," the reporter said, introducing himself, *"New York Daily Bulletin.* Strongman—er, Mr. van Norton—"

"Strongman is fine when I'm in uniform," the hero interjected.

"Strongman," Schreiber acknowledged. "Aren't you also concerned about reprisals against your family, like you said that Nucleus is?"

"You may have heard of the van Nortons," Strongman said, eliciting chuckles from the crowd; his family was well known for its wealth and its position in the city's history. "My family has had private security since before I was born. The danger to my family is minimal; certainly, not much greater than it ever was already. I can afford to be open about my identity in ways that some other heroes cannot." More laughs came from a few people, who caught his unintentional double-entendre. Strongman chuckled as well, realizing what he had said, then pointed to another reporter.

"Margaret Jameson, the *Times*," she said, introducing herself. She was tall, thin, and had dark brown hair, and wore a heavy, fur-lined winter coat with a matching fur-lined hat. Strongman could see the bottom of a dark blue dress emerging from beneath the coat. "Some have called you and the other new superheroes 'vigilantes,'" Jameson began. "How do you respond to that?"

"That's a valid concern," Strongman agreed, "but while I can't speak for other heroes, I will say that Nucleus and I work very hard to remain within the law. We cooperate with the police, and we are aware of the limitations we face as private citizens. It has worked well for us so far." As Jameson scribbled furiously in her notebook, Strongman pointed to another reporter.

"Joe Gordon," the reporter introduced himself, "the *Post*." Gordon was short and stocky, and wore a tan coat of a dark suit. He also sported a fedora, though his was dark brown. He quickly launched into his question. "How did you get your powers?"

"I wish," Strongman said with a grin, "that I could say that I studied a secret book of yogi exercises and honed my body to perfection, but the truth is, they just showed up one day when I was in Korea. One minute, I'm your average soldier, the next, I have the strength of a hundred elephants, skin as tough as a rhinoceros, and the speed of a racing car."

— § —

"Well, that went well," Strongman sighed as he and Nucleus stepped into a private room inside city hall.

"That description of your powers," Nucleus began, "was a bit...*florid*. Where did that come from?"

"I don't know," Strongman admitted. "Spur of the moment. It just came out."

"You *know* that's going to haunt you," Nucleus teased. "That quote is probably going to be in every paper." Strongman groaned. There was a knock on the door, and a moment later, a petite young woman with light brown hair and horn-rimmed glasses opened the door slightly, peeking her head in through the narrow opening.

"Excuse me, gentlemen," she said in a quiet voice. "The mayor would like to see you before you leave." She backed out of the doorway, indicating with a nod that she wanted them to follow her.

The two heroes proceeded into the hallway, and were met by a small crowd of gaping civil servants who were making their way through the building as they walked. Dozens of people stopped whatever it was that they were doing, and conversations came to abrupt stops as people noticed the superheroes in their midst. They went up stairs, through a maze of hallways, and eventually found themselves at the door to the mayor's office. Strongman knew that there was a faster, more direct route, and he suspected that either the mayor was stalling to prepare for the meeting, or someone wanted to show off that they were in the building. Perhaps both. Another possibility, petty though it was, was that the mayor wanted to demonstrate his power by making them jump through hoops for a task as simple as going to his office. The mayor had only recently taken office, and Strongman didn't know whether he was the kind of man to do something like that or not.

The trio stepped into the antechamber to the mayor's office—a room that featured a desk for the mayor's secretary, and several comfortable-looking chairs for guests to use while waiting to see him. The mayor's secretary, having escorted them this far, turned to face the heroes.

"Please wait here," she said, holding up a hand at waist level in a "stop" gesture. "I'll let the mayor know that you're here." She turned and stepped through the doorway to the mayor's office. Nucleus and Strongman exchanged glances for a moment, then the secretary returned, stopping in the doorway. "The mayor will see you now," she informed the two heroes. She stepped aside, her hand remaining on the doorknob as she held the door open for them. The two men stepped into the mayor's office, and the secretary closed the door behind them.

The mayor, standing behind his desk as Nucleus and Strongman entered the office, stepped out and around the desk, extending a hand to the heroes, a broad smile spreading across his face. Mayor Robert F. Wagner Jr. had only been in office for a month, having succeeded Mayor Impellitteri, and had dark, tightly-groomed hair that he kept in a short, conservative style.

"It's a pleasure to meet you, gentlemen," Wagner said, clasping Nucleus' hand and shaking it firmly. He did the same with Strongman, then indicated the sofa across from his desk. "Please," he said, "have a seat."

As the heroes sat on the sofa, carefully positioning their capes to avoid them becoming caught on the furniture, Wagner took a seat in one of the two chairs opposite the sofa. He looked at the heroes, still smiling, as they took their seats.

"Would you care for something to drink?" Wagner asked, indicating a tray on the coffee table between the sofa and the chairs; it held three glasses and a crystal decanter filled with an amber liquid.

"No, thank you," Nucleus said, holding out a gloved hand. Strongman shook his head with a small smile. The mayor nodded, and leaned back in his chair.

"Thank you for meeting with me," Wagner said pleasantly, crossing his right leg over his left and clasping his hands in his lap.

"Thank you for inviting us," Strongman replied. His background made him more comforable in these types of situations than Nucleus, who was having only limited success hiding his nervousness.

"Yes, thank you," Nucleus added.

"I invited you for a couple of reasons," Wagner said, answering the heroes' unspoken question. "First, I wanted to meet you." He spread his hands with a grin and a small shrug, then clasped them in his lap once more. "There's also a small matter of legalities." Nucleus and Strongman glanced nervously at one another. The mayor raised his hands in a placating gesture. "Nothing bad, I assure you. The two of you have done a tremendous amount of good for the city, and I want to find a way to keep that going."

"So do we, Mr. Mayor," Strongman agreed.

"First," Wagner continued, nodding, "you're not police. You seem to understand that point."

"Very much so, sir," Nucleus said. Wagner nodded again.

"The simplest solution," Wagner said, "would be to put you on the police force, but I have a feeling that wouldn't work for you."

"Not especially," Nucleus concurred.

"This is not something that we have to solve today," Wagner said, "but we do need to consider the matter carefully as we move forward. We're in unprecedented times."

"Yes, sir," Strongman agreed.

"This is less a concern for you, Strongman," Wagner began, "now that you have gone public with your identity, but anyone who wishes to remain anonymous will undoubtedly face trouble with the courts, eventually. If called to testify, for example, you will have few options: ignore the summons and become a fugitive; refuse to unmask and be held in contempt, at which point you'll face arrest and forcible unmasking; or comply and go on the record with your identity, like Strongman has." Nucleus frowned. He was trying to protect the people that he cared about, but he didn't want to break the law at the same time. There had to be a solution, but he couldn't think of it.

"There are other issues as well," Wagner continued. "Liability. Insurance. How do we contact you? Who do you work with? Do you become contract workers? The lawyers keep coming up with new questions." Nucleus and Strongman shifted uncomfortably in their seats. "As I said, we don't need to find the answers right now, but we do need to keep these questions in mind."

"Perhaps," Strongman suggested, "there's a way to establish a hero's identity with the city that lets them maintain a secret identity as far as the public is concerned."

"That is one angle," Wagner confirmed, "that the city attorney's office is pursuing."

"And for the moment, at least," Strongman continued, "you can reach us through my estate."

"Excellent," Wagner said.

"You've certainly given us a lot to think about," Strongman said. He stood and extended a hand across the coffee table toward the mayor. Wagner rose and took Strongman's hand. "Thank you for inviting us to see you." They shook hands firmly.

"It was a pleasure," Wagner said, then released his grip as Nucleus rose from the sofa. They clasped hands and exchanged a firm handshake as well. "We'll be in touch," the mayor added.

The heroes stepped toward the door, which opened moments before they reached it. Either the mayor's secretary had been listening in to know when she would again be needed, or she was psychic. *Maybe both,* Strongman joked to himself. They stepped into the antechamber, and Strongman winked at the attractive young woman with a sly grin as he passed her, but her face remained schooled to a neutral, businesslike expression. *Tough crowd,* Strongman thought.

Leaving the mayor's office unaccompanied, Nucleus and Strongman instead took the direct route to the building's exit. Within a few relatively short minutes, they were once again outside, on the steps of city hall. The crowd from the press conference had long since dispersed after the heroes went inside, and only the regular pedestrian traffic passed them on the sidewalk. Someone had already removed the podium that had been set up for their use.

Strongman nodded to Nucleus, then crouched and shot into the sky. The air around Nucleus' hands and feet shimmered and crackled, his bones visible through the glow in his extremities. He launched into the air after his friend, and they began to make their way across the city.

It was a beautiful day. The air was downright frigid as they soared through the skies, but Strongman barely noticed, with his near-invulnerable hide, and Nucleus had long since figured out how to fine-tune the control of his plasma to create a bubble of heated air around himself. The sun was shining brightly, with only a handful of puffy white clouds in the sky, and it reflected off of the rippling waters around the city.

CHAPTER THIRTEEN
Sunday, February 14, 1954

Evelyn and Alex picked at their dinner plates. As had been the case nearly every time they went out, the subject of the new superheroes had come up in one way or another. Their conversations then became confrontations, and a general bitterness was descending upon them.

Alex had decided that there was only one way to resolve this situation: he had to tell Evelyn that he was Nucleus. She knew that he supported the heroes in general, and Nucleus in particular, but he couldn't give her a good reason *why* without telling her about his double life. They had been together for too long, and had been through too much together for him to be anything less than honest with her. He was sure that, if she knew that he was one of the new heroes, then she would come around. She knew him. She could trust him.

Alex looked up from his plate of spaghetti and smiled weakly at Evelyn. She absently spun her fork in her pasta and smiled back, though her smile was equally strained. They sat in a modest restaurant in Manhattan that was decorated in shades of red, white, and pink, with strings of red bunting with heart shapes that spanned the curtain rods atop the windows.

Alex raised the glass of champagne that had been placed next to his water glass, to the right of his plate. "To us," he toasted. "Happy Valentine's Day."

Evelyn's smile began to spread to her eyes, becoming more genuine. She set down her fork and raised her glass. "To us," she echoed the toast. They extended their glasses, reaching across the table. The rims of the champagne flutes clicked with a high-pitched "tink" as the couple tapped them together. Evelyn and Alex sipped the effervescent liquid, then set their glasses back down on the table.

—$—

Percy van Norton sat in one of the overstuffed chairs in his study, the window shades opened to the wintry scene before him. He had a book open in his lap, but his attention wandered frequently from his reading. Van Norton rose and stepped over to the window. It was a beautiful evening, and he stood silently beside the window for several minutes, taking it in. There was a light coating of snow on the ground, and the lights of Manhattan were visible in the distance, beyond the trees that lined the perimeter of his family's property.

Movement along the trees caught his eye. He watched intently, standing as still as possible to avoid being seen... just in case. He saw the shape of a man in dark clothing, staying close to the shadows. *Black Cobra?* van Norton wondered, remembering the vigilante hero's methods, but then he saw another man.

And another.

And another.

His home was under attack, van Norton realized. He stepped back, away from the window, and made his way briskly toward the door to the study. He all but ran down the hall to the staircase that led to the ground floor. Grabbing the banister, he heaved himself over, and came to a thunderous landing at the foot of the stairs. Picture frames and other decorations swayed from the vibration of his landing. One of the stewards turned in shock at van Norton's abrupt descent. "M-master Percy?" he stammered.

"Get my parents and the staff to the safe room," van Norton ordered, "and alert the guards. The house is under attack. There's at least four men on the south lawn." The steward nodded, the blood draining from his face. Van Norton jogged to the doors leading outside. He paused as he stepped out into the cold February evening. He looked around, taking stock of his surroundings and evaluating his situation, like he'd been trained to do in the Army, and practiced for more than a year in Korea.

Van Norton caught a glimpse of movement to his left. Someone had darted across part of the lawn, their black clothing in sharp contrast to the white snow. The man was trying to move from one place of concealment to another, but van Norton had spotted him in the last instant. He vaulted into the air, his trajectory calculated through training and practice during his time at Fort Leonard Wood, and came down almost on top of the intruder.

The intruder cried out in a language that van Norton didn't understand as he brought a rifle to bear on the hero. Automatic weapons fire erupted from the man's weapon, which van Norton's trained eye quickly identified as a Kalashnikov, a Russian-made AK-47. The bullets bounced off van Norton's skin, shredding the loose shirt he'd been wearing in the process.

"Mein Gott!" the intruder yelled, his eyes widening in shock. He continued firing as van Norton grabbed the hot barrel of the rifle, wrenched it out of the man's hands, and tossed it aside. *"Stirbst du nicht?"*

That sounds like German, van Norton thought. He grabbed the intruder by the scruff of his collar, and pulled him close to his face. He made his voice an intimidating growl and demanded, "Who are you? Who do you work for?"

"Ni-nichts verstehen," the intruder whimpered, his feet dangling several inches off of the ground. *"Bitte... bitte tu mir nicht weh."*

Van Norton sighed. He had no idea what the man was saying. He raised a fist above the terrified man's head, to a cry of *"Nein!"* He brought his hand down fast and hard, rendering the man unconscious. The man slumped in van Norton's grip, and the hero set the unconscious intruder down on the ground. While the language barrier had prevented him from interrogating the man, he had learned something: the man's clothes smelled of seawater and fish. He'd come from the docks.

—§—

Donner checked his watch, then put it back into the pocket of his coat. He remembered the harsh winters in Germany as a child, but nearly a decade of living in South America had acclimated him to milder temperatures. He pulled the heavy coat tighter around him. The assault on the opulent home of Strongman should have begun already. The man had been a fool to reveal not only his identity, but also the extent of his powers openly like he had a week before. The assault on his home was a last-minute addition to the plan, but it should distract him and keep him away from the main thrust of the attack, which Donner would personally lead into the heart of the city.

The Soviet Kalashnikov rifles he had acquired should have no trouble penetrating the "skin as tough as a rhinoceros," and the explosives they carried were enough to turn the building into flaming rubble. There were other *übermenschen* that he would have to deal with, true, but this would eliminate one of the most powerful in the opening moments of the attack on the city.

Without bothering to turn around, he addressed his lieutenants, who were standing directly behind him. "It is time," he said. "Begin the operation." The men turned crisply to issue orders to the crowd of men behind them. They were all standing on the deck of the small freighter that had brought them here from Buenos Aires over the past month. Within minutes, the heavily-armed force had disembarked and was marching up the all-but deserted dock, headed directly for Manhattan.

— § —

Alex Stevens had prepared for this moment, but his stomach still churned, now that the time was approaching. He had even worn his uniform under the dress clothes that he had picked out for this special Valentine's dinner with Evelyn. His mask was in his pocket, along with a small bottle of spirit gum.

"I know this is an uncomfortable subject for us," Alex began, "but I want you to understand why I support the heroes like I do." Evelyn's expression soured. She would rather not talk about the subject at all.

"Can we talk about it another time?" she asked after a moment, exasperated. "It's Valentine's Day. Can't we just have a nice dinner without bringing... *them* into it?"

"I'm sorry," Alex said, "but this is important."

Evelyn threw her napkin on the table and stood quickly, anger in her eyes. "No," she said. "Not today. Not here. Not now. *We* are important. Those *fr*— those... *people*," she spat the word out, clearly having substituted the harsher epithet at the last moment, "are not! Until you can see that, don't talk to me." She turned and stormed out of the restaurant before Alex could have a chance to reply or even rise more than halfway out of his seat.

As he slumped back into his chair, their waiter returned to the table. *He saw the whole thing*, Alex thought, mortified. Then the realization dawned on him that, if he'd managed to tell Evelyn his secret before she'd stormed out, and she still reacted as she just had, she might have blurted it out in anger. The waiter stepped over and put a sympathetic hand on his shoulder, then said, "Sorry, son." He smiled and added, "Don't worry about the bill."

"I," Alex began, flummoxed. "Thanks."

"You got enough bad news for one night," the waiter said. "Least I could do."

Alex collected his hat and coat and left the restaurant. He didn't see Evelyn outside anywhere. *She must have taken a cab*, he thought; they had come together in one. Alex started walking, aimlessly. He had only been walking for a few minutes when he was greeted by the sound of screams and automatic weapons fire.

Alex ducked into a nearby alley. Quickly doffing his clothing, he stood in his uniform. He pulled his mask out, applied a small amount of the spirit gum, and placed it onto his face. He grabbed his clothing, then looked around. He had no idea where to put his clothes. As he looked desperately for a spot to hide his clothes where they wouldn't potentially be stolen, he realized where he was: Steel Sterling's office building.

He flew up, and quickly found the fire escape located at the window of Sterling's office. He landed on the steel platform, and set his bundle of clothing down. He stepped over to the window and peered in. The office was dark, and no one appeared to be in. Sterling probably wasn't back from Brazil yet. Getting help from a man with Sterling's powers would have been helpful, but it appeared to be out of the question. Leaving his clothes on the platform, Nucleus lifted off into the sky to get a better view and figure out what was going on.

— § —

Van Norton slammed his fist into the side of another black-clad intruder's head, pulling his punch so it would render him unconscious, rather than kill the man outright by pulverizing his skull. Gunfire sounded off to his right; his guards were engaged in a running battle with the intruders, who numbered at least six by van Norton's updated count. The guards' pistols were no match for the Kalashnikovs carried by the attackers, but they had evened the playing field by turning the rifles against the attackers as each one was captured.

Disarming the unconscious man, he leaped toward the sound of the gunfire. He dropped the rifle and ammunition he'd taken from the intruder as his leap took him over one of the guards, and the arc of his travel deposited him in front of this attacker. His body now shielding the guard, who was already arming himself with the rifle, the attacker fired uselessly at van Norton as he stalked forward.

Van Norton rendered the attacker unconscious as easily as he had the others, then disarmed him. He stood and listened. The sounds of weapons fire had stopped. Another guard, now also armed with a captured Kalashnikov, came running in his direction.

"The grounds are secure, sir," the guard reported, panting. "We count six hostiles, including the two you just took down. Two were killed in the fight. Three of ours were wounded, and one dead." He paused. "These guys were *good*. They would have taken us by surprise without your warning."

"I was lucky," van Norton said. "I happened to look out the window at just the right time."

"We have two hostiles that we captured over here, sir," the guard said, indicating the direction he'd just come from.

"Take me to them," van Norton said, hefting the unconscious form of the man he'd just fought with over his shoulder. The pair walked over to a well-lit section of the grounds. The two prisoners sat, their hands bound behind them, against a wall. They glowered up at the guards standing watch over them, now armed with the same rifles they'd brought to carry out their attack. Their gear had been stripped from them, and lay in a pile several yards away, where another guard was examining it. Van Norton dropped the man he was carrying near the other two, and another of the guards stepped forward to place his arms in restraints before he regained consciousness.

The guard who accompanied van Norton spoke to one of the other guards. "There's one more," he said, indicating the direction that he and van Norton had come from, "back that way, near Jones. Help him secure the prisoner and bring him over here with the others." The other guard nodded and took off at a jog.

"They won't talk," one of the guards reported. "They act like they don't even speak English."

"They probably don't," van Norton said. "I heard one of them speaking German."

"German?" one of the older guards said, surprised. "I ain't fought Krauts in almost ten years."

"Anybody here speak German?" van Norton asked. "I have some questions that need answers."

"I speak a little German," one of the younger guards, who was standing a few yards away from everyone else, said nervously. "I mean, I took some German in high school."

"Better than us," van Norton said. "You're hired." The young guard moved over by the others. "Ask them who they are, and who they work for."

The young man, who van Norton could now see was barely out of high school and probably just had his first taste of anything resembling combat, turned to the prisoners and relayed van Norton's questions in halting German.

For several moments, the prisoners sat in defiant silence. Then, van Norton stepped forward, eying the first of the men he'd taken down. In the light, van Norton could see that he was barely more than a kid, probably about the same age as their impromptu translator. He could see the fear in the kid's eyes. Keeping his face a stony mask, he narrowed his eyes, and cracked the knuckles of his fists. It worked like a charm. The kid broke instantly.

"He says his name is Johann Schmidt," the young guard translated, trying not to laugh. "No, really."

"Who's Johann Schmidt?" one of the other guards asked, confused.

"That's the Red Skull's real name," the young guard replied. "From Captain America." The other guards laughed out loud.

"Who's his boss?" van Norton asked. The kid repeated the question in German.

"He said he's..." he trailed off, dumbfounded, as Schmidt replied in rapid German.

"Did I just hear that kid say 'Reich?'" the older guard asked, starting to raise his rifle to bear on the prisoners.

Van Norton waved for the guard to stand down. "What did he say?" he pressed.

"He said," the young guard began, translating uncertainly, "that they're working for *Thor* to restore the Reich. I... I must have gotten that wrong."

"Thor?" van Norton asked.

"Well, Donner," the young guard said. "It's the German name for Thor. It literally means 'thunder.'"

"Ask him about this 'Donner,'" van Norton instructed the young guard. "It's probably some sort of code name."

The guard translated as instructed, then after the young German spoke, he said, "Donner is the leader of their group. He's an... he's like you, sir. A superhuman."

"Where is he?" van Norton asked. As soon as the guard translated the question, the other prisoner began yelling at his young peer.

"He's telling him not to answer," the young guard translated, un-asked.

"I figured as much," van Norton said. He picked the older German up, then smacked his head, leaving him dazed... and quiet. Van Norton glared at the young prisoner, who immediately began talking almost as fast as he could manage to get the words out. Before the translator could interpret the young prisoner's words, van Norton had already picked out the word that he needed: Manhattan.

Chapter Fourteen

Flying to the roof of the office building, Nucleus perched over the ledge, looking for the source of the gunfire. The sound echoed off the walls of the buildings like a concrete canyon, making it hard to pinpoint. The crowds of fleeing civilians, on the other hand...

Spotting the group of black-clad men armed with automatic rifles was fairly simple after that. They were employing some fairly sophisticated urban warfare techniques, and were obviously well-armed. At the forefront of the group, one man seemed oddly unarmed... until a lightning bolt shot from his hand.

Several dozen heavily-armed men, plus one superhuman with a powerful distance attack, against a handful of police and one super-hero who *wasn't bulletproof.*

I've got this, Nucleus thought. *I hope.*

Having changed quickly out of his shredded clothes into a—slightly—more durable uniform, Strongman bounded toward Manhattan, each leap taking him further than he'd ever gone before. Each time he hit the ground, he turned the landing into a crouch, which he then used to immediately leap once more.

As he neared Manhattan's wharf, he could hear faint screams and the sound of automatic weapons fire. He scanned the area, and a familiar glow caught his eye: Nucleus was already there, flying onto the roof of a building. He changed direction with his next leap, and slowed his pace.

Strongman landed on the opposite side of the roof from Nucleus. The other hero's attention was on the streets below, and the din of battle was growing, so the crunch of Strongman's boots on the paved roofing material went unheard. Strongman walked toward his friend, who appeared to be steeling himself for a fight.

"How bad is it?" Strongman asked. Nucleus whipped around into a fighting stance, having been caught unawares. He relaxed when he recognized Strongman.

"Thank God you're here," Nucleus said, the relief palpable in his voice. "There's about fifty men, all heavily armed, making their way inland from the docks. I'm not sure I could get through that much gunfire, but you can. They're being led by a superhuman who can shoot lightning bolts from his hands."

"Donner," Strongman noted.

"What?" Nucleus asked.

"His name," Strongman said, "is Donner. He sent six men to blow up my house and kill me." Nucleus' eyes widened. "Obviously, *that* didn't go too well for them. They're Germans, and they want to bring back the Reich. Oh, and his name? It's German for Thor. He thinks he's the second coming."

Nucleus blew out a breath he didn't realize he had been holding. This was insane—*literally* insane—on so many levels.

"So," Strongman asked, "got a plan?"

— § —

Donner laughed. This was simply too easy. None of the *übermenschen* had shown their faces to oppose him, and the police were all but totally impotent in the face of his power. He fired another lightning bolt, which struck a police car. The car exploded, sending flames and debris shooting in every direction. The police officers standing near the car were thrown in the air. They landed hard, and their uniforms were on fire.

Suddenly, something slammed into the ground behind him, in the midst of his men. Donner spun, and narrowly avoided a blast of energy that shot past him, where he had been standing a moment earlier.

So, Donner thought, *the* übermenschen *have arrived at last.* He grinned ferociously. In front of him, he could see Nucleus descending from on high, his cape billowing in the wind. Behind him, Strongman tore into his men with a ferocity that Donner couldn't help but admire. Clearly, his assault on Strongman's home had been a failure. He had underestimated the hero, and he vowed not to do so again.

Donner dodged as Nucleus fired several more blasts of energy in his direction. He returned fire, hurling bolts of lightning at the airborne *übermensch*, who ducked and weaved through the air with ease, never remaining still or traveling in a straight line long enough to present a clear target.

A third figure rocketed toward the ground from the heavens like a stone. Donner easily struck him with a lightning bolt. It had no effect. The form continued inexorably toward him, taking several more bolts of lighting, equally ineffectually.

The form slammed into Donner, sending him flying through his men, halfway down the block from where they had come. A cloud of disturbed snow and debris rose from the force of the impact. As it settled, Steel Sterling stood, fists clenched, over Donner, who lay on his back at Sterling's feet.

Sterling wore a simple red t-shirt and a pair of blue denim pants, with a pair of black, military-style boots. His blond hair was disheveled, and his piercing blue eyes glared at Donner. "Stay down," Sterling warned.

"No," Donner replied in heavily-accented English. "I will not." He suddenly reached toward Sterling and unleashed another bolt of lightning, which struck the hero squarely in the chest. Sterling didn't even move.

"That," Sterling said after a moment, "tickled."

Donner's eyes widened in surprise. Sterling reached down and grabbed Donner by his coat. Sterling lifted the German, holding him up so that their eyes met, and their faces nearly touched.

"I'm taking you in," Sterling growled. "You've hurt enough people for one day."

Donner grinned. "I think not," he said. "I have only just begun."

Before Sterling could reply, a bullet ricocheted off of his forehead. As his attention shifted to find where the shot had come from, Donner punched Sterling hard in the face. Though it didn't hurt, it was unexpected and gave Donner the opportunity that he needed to slip out of his coat and escape Sterling's grasp.

Nucleus watched as Donner scrambled away from Steel Sterling. He raised a hand, preparing to fire an energy blast at the Nazi villain, but just as Donner began to lift into the air, a hail of *arrows* began to fall around the Nazi. Though he managed to avoid most of them, largely due to his unexpectedly taking flight, one struck him in the leg, burying itself in his calf.

Yelping in pain, Donner rocketed into the sky and out of sight. Nucleus swore under his breath. He looked around, trying to find the person responsible for firing the arrows. A glimpse of movement on a nearby rooftop caught his eye, and Nucleus launched himself after it as Strongman and Steel Sterling grappled with Donner's foot soldiers in the street.

Nucleus landed on the roof, and saw two men fighting, engaged in an evenly-matched hand-to-hand battle. He recognized the black-clad figure as the Black Cobra. He dodged and weaved, striking out with his feet and fists in a blur of motion as he avoided a series of similar strikes from a man in a deep-red, hooded outfit, a matching bow in his hands and a red quiver of arrows on his back. A red mask covered half of the man's face. The scarlet archer used the bow like a staff, striking out with it, but his blows failed to land on their targets. Nucleus watched the fight for several seconds, then fired a burst of energy between the two combatants.

"That's enough!" Nucleus shouted. "Stand down, both of you!" Startled, the two men paused in their fighting stances and looked at Nucleus. He didn't give them an opportunity to resume their fight or to force him to join in. "What the hell is going on here?" he demanded. He looked at the archer. "Donner got away, thank you very much, and his men are still down there... and yet, you two idiots are up here fighting each other, instead of the literal *Nazis* in the street!"

The archer looked abashed, while the Black Cobra's expression remained unreadable. "I didn't expect him to fly off," the archer said quietly. "Those should have taken him down for good."

"Like hell you're using lethal force on my watch," Nucleus said, a hint of menace in his voice. "You are *not* judge, jury, and executioner!"

"That maniac was shooting *lightning* bolts!" the archer shot back. "The police couldn't stop him!"

"But *we* can," Nucleus replied. "Steel Sterling and I nearly had him." The archer scoffed. "For now, both of you get down there and help. This conversation is not over, Arrow." Nucleus turned and leaped off the edge of the building, his feet and hands instantly igniting with plasma, carrying him safely away. The Black Cobra eyed the archer with distrust, then turned and leaped off another side of the building, adjacent to the next building over. He caromed off the walls and fire escape ladders and platforms, spinning and whirling as he descended to ground level.

The archer watched the Black Cobra as he descended, sneering. "Show off," he muttered, then began to climb down the ladder. By the time he reached the ground, the fighting was all but over. *Clearly*, he thought, *I need a faster way to travel.* He kicked one of the Nazi foot soldiers, who had begun to stir as he walked nearby.

More police officers had arrived on scene, and were beginning to collect the small army of defeated Nazis, while paramedics loaded injured police officers into an ambulance. The archer joined a nervous Black Cobra near Nucleus and Strongman, while Steel Sterling helped wrangle the unconscious men into a waiting police wagon.

"We can't thank you enough," a man in a suit was saying, "for your assistance this evening." It took a moment before the archer recognized him as Mayor Wagner. "This was a bit beyond the usual capabilities of the New York Police Department, and you rose to the challenge and came to their aid just in time." He looked at the archer and the Black Cobra, his head tilted slightly to one side. "I don't believe I've met these two gentlemen yet."

"Mr. Mayor," Strongman said, "I believe you may have heard of the Black Cobra." He indicated the black-clad hero with a wave of his hand, then looked toward the archer, his brow furrowing. "I haven't had the pleasure," he said to the archer, his voice trailing off expectantly.

The archer cleared his throat, thankful for the hood and mask that obscured his features. "Nucleus called me the Arrow," he said. "I guess that will do." The mayor nodded.

"I see," the mayor said. "I'm glad to have you all here, fighting the good fight."

Chapter Fifteen
Tuesday, February 16, 1954

Alex Stevens sat in the living room with his parents and sister. They all watched the television, which was tuned to the evening news broadcast. On the screen was the NBC news anchor John Cameron Swayze; he had dark hair that was brushed to the side of a widow's peak, and was wearing a gray suit. On the wall behind him was a map of the world, and on the table before him was a stack of papers, a small microphone, and a pair of glasses.

"It's been two days," Swayze said on the screen, "since the Valentine's Day attack on Manhattan. The attackers have been identified as German Nazis who had fled to South America following the end of the Second World War. They were led by Erich Eidelmann, who prefers to be called Donner, the German name for the ancient Norse god, Thor." The image on the screen changed, displaying a picture of Donner taken during the attack, as Swayze continued speaking. "Donner, the son of a former Nazi general, is a superhuman, and apparently possesses the ability to shoot bolts of lightning and to fly." The image on the screen changed again, returning to a shot of Swayze at his news desk.

"Donner," Swayze continued, "was stopped by five of New York City's new heroes: Nucleus, Strongman, Steel Sterling, the Black Cobra, and the Arrow. Though Donner escaped, the city is in their debt. Donner remains at large, as well as several of his accomplices. They are considered armed and extremely dangerous, and should not be approached."

"Thank God for Nucleus," Alex's father began, "and the other heroes. *Nazis*. Here. In New York." He shook his head regretfully. Alex leaned forward in his chair, clearing his throat. His father looked at him, his brow furrowed quizzically. "You have something to add, son?" he asked.

"Yes, actually," Alex said. "I've got something I've been meaning to tell all of you for a while." He rose and stood in front of the television. He raised his right hand, bending his arm at the elbow to keep his hand just above waist level. He looked at his hand, and activated his powers. His hand began to glow. His mother gasped, and his sister, Megan, squealed. "I'm," he began.

"You're Nucleus!" Megan interrupted, excited.

As Alex extinguished the glow of plasma around his hand, he realized that his father hadn't reacted as strongly as his mother or sister to the news. He shared a look with his father, then asked, "You knew?"

"Only recently," his father said. "I suspected at first, then more strongly until a couple weeks ago."

"What gave it away?" Alex asked. His father was quiet for a moment, gathering his thoughts. Alex's mother and Megan stared at him in surprise; they hadn't realized the truth at all.

"Nucleus first showed up right after you got back from the war," his father began. "You were evasive when I asked about your experiences, but I thought that could have just been shell shock, and that you'd come around in time. Then there was that injury you had right about the same time that Nucleus disappeared for a few weeks. When your friend Percy announced that he was Strongman, that's when I knew."

"You never said anything," Alex said.

"What was there to say?" his father asked. "You were doing what you thought was best to protect your community with the gifts that you've been given. I think it's obvious that you and Percy were in Team Liberty together." Everyone was quiet for a few moments. "I'm proud of you, son," his father said. Megan stood and gave her brother a bear hug, then was joined by their parents.

— § —

Jim Hornsby and his brother Bob sparred in a medium-sized basement room. The floor was a bare concrete slab with a threadbare carpet under their feet at the center of the room. Lamps in each corner and a fifth suspended from a wooden slat at the center of the ceiling kept the room brightly lit. The walls were bare concrete, and there were no windows. A single flight of battered wooden stairs led to the floor above. A pair of old wooden chairs stood along the wall adjacent to the stairway, a towel draped across the back of one, and another balled up on the seat of the other. Next to the chairs sat a pair of bags with a change of clothing inside, and their shoes sat next to the bags. A small end table held two glasses of water, condensation dripping down their sides and pooling around their bases.

Bob blocked a series of rapid kicks and punches, then effortlessly took the offensive, responding in kind. His blows were likewise deflected by Jim. This back-and-forth sparring continued for several minutes.

"Enough," Jim said, stepping back. He and Bob faced one another, then bowed deeply and rigidly from the waist, their arms kept stiffly at their sides. When they straightened once more, Jim relaxed and said, "Well done, Bob. You're picking this up faster than I'd expected." The two brothers stepped over to the chairs and began to wipe the sweat from their faces with their towels. Bob grabbed a glass and took a deep drink of water.

"Thanks," Bob said after a moment. "I want to get out there to help you."

"I understand," Jim said, "but you're not ready yet. You still have a lot to learn."

"But I," Bob began.

"Patience," Jim interrupted. "It took me *years* to learn what I know. You've only been at this for a few weeks. You're not ready yet." Bob visibly suppressed an angry retort; he knew that Jim was right, even if he didn't want to accept it. Jim clapped him on the shoulder. "Break's over," he said, and led Bob back onto the carpeted area of their makeshift dojo. As they began practicing their forms, Jim asked, "Have you given any thought to what you want to do after high school?"

"I was thinking," Bob began, contorting his arms and legs from one position to another as he spoke, "about something in law enforcement at the federal level. Maybe the FBI or the U.S. Marshals."

Jim raised an eyebrow in surprise. "I hadn't expected that," he admitted. "I thought you didn't want to go into the law."

"I don't want to be a *lawyer*," Bob clarified. "This is different." Jim nodded, and the two brothers resumed sparring in relative silence.

— § —

The car careened through traffic, fishtailing as it rounded an intersection at high speed. The rear bumper of the car slammed into another vehicle, but the driver ignored the collision and increased speed. An instant later, Strongman bounded through the intersection in pursuit. Strongman continued in his original direction, however, not turning where the car had turned. With another leap, he landed on the roof of a nearby building. He could tell that the car was headed for the waterfront, and he wanted to make the men inside the car believe that they had lost him, in order to follow them from a distance and discover their destination. Jumping from rooftop to rooftop, Strongman let the car gain some distance, while his change in altitude allowed him to to keep an eye on the car.

The car weaved more slowly through several blocks before approaching the docks, apparently hoping to throw off any further pursuit. Ultimately, the car came to a stop beside a small freighter. After a moment, the car's occupants got out and made their way up the gangway, and boarded the ship.

Strongman quietly made his way down near the freighter. There were several crates marked "agricultural machinery" on the dock, either having been recently unloaded or were waiting to be loaded aboard the vessel. Something about all of this seemed off to Strongman, however. Prying open one of the crates, he realized immediately that it was anything but farming equipment. If anything, it was some sort of artillery piece. Before he could look any further, however, Strongman heard a snapping sound from above. A crane had been repositioned while he was searching, and someone had just used it to drop a massive steel boiler on top of him!

Throwing his hands up above his head, Strongman braced himself. An instant later, the boiler slammed into him. The concrete of the dock cracked and buckled under his feet, and the metal of the boiler deformed around his hands, but he managed to catch the enormous metal cylinder. With a grunt, Strongman heaved the boiler into the air.

It soared up, arced over the freighter, and crashed into the water on the opposite side.

With a leap, Strongman vaulted onto the deck of the freighter. He heard a voice cry out in German as he landed, and several men came at him. He easily batted them aside, one after another. A half dozen men from the ship's crew, their desperation rising, came forward with a hose. Pain shot through Strongman as a torrent of superheated steam struck him. Overcome, he lost consciousness and fell to the deck.

The sailors rushed forward. Wincing at first, as Strongman was incredibly hot to the touch, albeit only slightly reddened from the torrent of steam that would have burned a normal man to death in seconds, they used heavy chains to lash him to one of the anchors on the deck, which had not been used while the ship was docked. Once secured, they worked together to lift the bound hero, and heaved him over the side of the ship.

The shock of the frigid seawater woke Strongman upon immersion. He flexed his muscles, and with a minimum of effort, shattered the chain that had, moments earlier, held him fast to the anchor that was quickly sinking to the bottom of the harbor.

Strongman swam under the freighter, where he found the chain of the anchor on the side opposite the dock. He began to climb, the large links making for easy hand- and foot-holds. As he climbed aboard the ship, he saw the crew peering over the deck, looking into the water where they had thrown him moments earlier. They were talking in boisterous German while laughing and slapping each other on the back.

Hiding behind a large object covered by a tarp, Strongman thought quickly. He needed to do something to incapacitate this ship. It could not be a coincidence that a bunch of Nazis showed up near the docks, while a ship crewed by Germans was smuggling some serious weaponry. Looking under the tarp, he saw another artillery piece, this one bolted down as a makeshift deck gun.

Quickly throwing the tarp aside, Strongman grabbed the barrel of the deck gun. Pulling hard, he ripped the gun free of its moorings with a screech of straining metal. Holding the enormous barrel like a giant baseball bat, he swung as the surprised crew turned and began to rush toward him. The crewmen were swept away by the giant club, and went flying across the deck. Strongman felt the ship begin to move, and heard snapping sounds coming from the dock. Running to the side of the ship, Strongman saw the ropes securing the ship to the dock pulling tightly, straining as the ship moved away, before the cleats bolted to the dock gave way, snapping out from the concrete and into the air. The gangway sheared away, and hung from the side of the ship at an odd angle.

As the ship picked up speed and moved away from the docks toward the open sea and the shipping lanes, Strongman turned back toward the ship's deck. He hefted the barrel once more, and began to swing it wildly, in order to cause as much damage as possible.

Minutes passed, and the deck was a disaster. Oddly, no one had opposed him. It was then that Strongman noticed where the crew was: they were climbing into the lifeboats, and abandoning ship. He knew that he hadn't done anything close to catastrophic damage to the ship, so that could only mean that they intended to scuttle the ship with him aboard in a last-ditch effort to kill him.

The ship began to rock not from the ocean waves, but from a series of explosions. Strongman hurled the makeshift club aside, and the barrel, now bent and misshapen, crashed into the water and sank. Strongman leaped from the deck as it began to erupt from the explosions that were consuming the ship from the inside out.

Strongman swam back to shore. He saw the bow of the ship slip under the surface as he stepped out of the surf and looked back.

— § —

Alex knocked on the door to Evelyn's apartment. After a moment, the door opened, and Evelyn's mother's face appeared in the doorway. She smiled broadly when she realized who was at the door. She was an attractive woman in her mid-forties, with brown hair in a conservative style, bright red lipstick that made her smile seem even brighter, and she wore a simple blue dress that nevertheless managed to accentuate her figure.

"Alex!" she practically sang, smiling broadly. "Come in! I haven't seen you in weeks!"

Alex smiled half-heartedly as he stepped through the doorway and into the apartment. "Evelyn and I," he began uncertainly.

"I know," she replied. "I hope you two can work out whatever it is that's come between you. You were always good together."

"Me too," Alex replied. "That's why I'm here."

"Evelyn is in her room," she said. "I'll go get her."

"Thank you," Alex said. Evelyn's mother turned and walked down the hall, knocking on the door near the far end.

"Evelyn," she said. "Honey, Alex is here to see you." Alex could hear the muffled sound of a chair moving, its feet scraping against the wooden floor. A moment later, the door opened slightly. Evelyn peered her head out. She looked past her mother, and glared at Alex.

"Can we talk?" Alex asked, speaking just loudly enough to be heard down the hallway. Evelyn stared at him silently for a long moment, and it made Alex uncomfortable. Over the past few weeks, he had come to realize that they had rarely disagreed when they were dating before he left for the war. Upon reflection, he realized that, almost always, he had been the one to relent to her stubborn streak. This was the first time that he *hadn't* given in to her.

"Will it matter?" she demanded, crossing her arms defiantly.

"I suppose that's up to you," Alex said. "Will you at least listen to what I have to say?"

"You keep saying the same thing," Evelyn replied. "So what's the point?"

Alex sighed, closing his eyes sadly. He had been afraid that it would come to this. "Then that's it," he said, almost too softly for her to hear him. "I tried." He turned, taking hold of the doorknob. "Goodbye, Evelyn." As Evelyn's mother watched in silent disbelief, Alex opened the door. He stepped outside, closed the door behind him, and began to make his way to the stairs. As he began his descent, he could hear raised, muffled voices coming from Evelyn's aparment.

— § —

John "Steel" Sterling stepped into the doorway of the warehouse. It was pitch black inside, and he moved cautiously, careful not to trip over anything. Following closely behind, his service revolver drawn and ready, was Officer Clancy of the New York Police Department.

Clancy, a twenty-five-year veteran of the police force, was a short, heavyset man in his mid-forties. His bright red hair was beginning to recede, giving him a pronounced widow's peak. His uniform was rumpled and ill-fitting, and his jowls sagged. He wore a serious expression on his face; his lips were pinched, and his eyebrows furrowed.

Clancy had worked with Sterling on several cases already, and the two had developed an easy working relationship, and the income generated by his fees as a consulting investigator for the New York Police Department was a welcome boost to his finances. As much as he disliked having Clancy interrupt a dinner date with Dora Cummings, he appreciated the business.

He'd met Dora on another case shortly after going into business, when her father, the famed scientist and industrialist Dr. Walter Cummings, had been kidnapped by someone calling himself Dr. Yar; that person had been revealed as the Black Knight he'd encountered on his first two cases, using a new alias. "Yar" had, once again, apparently been killed, but the madman had shown a frustrating penchant for defying the odds, and Sterling didn't want to write him off until he had more definitive proof.

Following that first meeting, their paths crossed several more times, as she and her father were targeted repeatedly by the Black Knight and other unsavory characters. Sterling had recently begun seeing Dora, and they had formed a quick bond.

Though he kept the barrel of his revolver pointed at the ground, Clancy's gun followed his gaze as his eyes swept the darkened warehouse. He held the butt of the pistol with both hands in a weaver stance, and hunched over slightly as he made his way forward, his eyes widening in the dark.

"This is the police!" Clancy announced to the darkened warehouse. "If anybody's there, come out now if ya know what's good for ya!" Sterling gave Clancy a sideways glance, then stepped past him. Reaching for the wall near the door, he grabbed a lever attached to a box with cables extending from the top. He flipped the switch, and it sparked for a moment as the contacts touched, then the lights began to flicker to life an instant later.

Sterling glanced around the warehouse once more as the lights slowly began to glow brighter and brighter. There were crates as far as the eye could see, stacked high in neat rows. He had joined Clancy for the investigation of this warehouse, which had been contracted to store the cargo shipped in there by freighter that attacked Strongman the day before, then scuttled itself. Clancy had no problem obtaining a search warrant, and Sterling was all too happy to lend his muscle, in case there were any more surprises like those that had found Strongman.

Sterling and Clancy made their way to the warehouse's office, located atop a mezzanine in a corner near the doorway they'd just come through. The door was locked, like that on the outside, but that didn't pose any difficulty for Sterling. Although he had come to realize that many of his powers were tuned to magnetism—he could cause himself to "stick" to metal, and he flew by pushing against the metal in the Earth's core, for example—he hadn't yet developed the fine control to pick a lock. What he *could* do, however, was magnetically force the locked deadbolt assembly back into the door, and twist the doorknob on the other side, bypassing the lock completely.

He pushed the door open, and Clancy whistled. "That's a mighty slick trick, Steel," the police officer commented. "Don't let me catch you usin' it without permission."

"I only use it at parties," Sterling shot back, grinning. He stepped through the door, and made his way to a file cabinet behind the desk that dominated the back of the small room. As Clancy began to sift through the folders and papers stacked on the desk, Sterling did the same with the folders in the filing cabinet. Several moments passed, then Clancy let loose an excited cry.

"Got it!" he announced. "The crates we're looking for are in Row 5, Section 12." Returning the papers, folders and drawers to where they'd found them, Sterling and Clancy exited the office and stepped back out into the warehouse. The two walked briskly to their destination, only to find an empty space, demarcated by faded lines of white paint on the concrete floor. A large "12" was painted in stencil at the front of the space.

"Where's it all at?" Clancy asked, doffing his cap and scratching his red hair.

"They must have quietly taken it somewhere else," Sterling said, "while everyone was swarming the crates still on the dock last night." He blew out a breath. "These guys are organized *and well-funded.*"

Sterling and Officer Clancy returned to the office. They found the paperwork for the shipment easily enough this time, but there was no record of it being removed from the warehouse. According to the paperwork, it was still in the process of being offloaded from the ship, which lined up with the crates found on the dock. The customs inspection hadn't even occurred yet, so there was truly no telling what was *really* in the crates that had been taken. According to the warehouse's copy of the manifest, it was "agricultural machinery" and "engine parts," with "textiles" and "foodstuffs." More than likeliy, it was weapons, explosives, uniforms, and rations. Nearly half of Donner's army had escaped on Sunday. It seemed a certainty that there was now a small army on the loose, and they were being led by a madman.

Chapter Sixteen

Friday, February 19, 1954

Pebbles of loose asphalt crunched under the tires of the large car as it slowed to a stop. It was late evening, and the car's exhaust was amplified by the cloud of steam it generated as it escaped into the cold winter air. A man jumped out from the front passenger seat, opening his door and shutting it again with quick efficiency. He briskly moved around the front of the car, stopping at the rear door on the opposite side. He grabbed the door handle, pulled the car door open, then stood at attention.

A man in a heavy coat, pressed suit, and impeccably-shined shoes stepped out, placing a wide-brimmed hat on his head as he exited the back seat of the car. Blond hair was visible as he adjusted the hat with his gloved hand before looking up.

Donner stepped forward, and was soon joined by two more men in similar attire. They moved to flank him, and as they began to walk toward the building to which their driver had brought them, the other man closed the car's door and quickly got back into his seat. The car pulled away, presumably for the driver to find a suitable place to park.

"Why did I let you talk me into this?" Donner muttered with disgust to the men at his sides. "We don't need help from these vermin."

The man to Donner's right sighed quietly, then said, "We do, *mein Herr*. They have an extensive underground network that we need." Donner furrowed his brow in disgust, but said nothing. The three men walked up the steps to the front door of the building. The man to Donner's right reached out and knocked. The door opened, and a young Asian man in a dark gray suit with a black necktie greeted them.

"Welcome, gentlemen," he said in lightly-accented English. He turned to another young Asian man, who looked to be barely out of his teenage years, and said, "Jason, take their coats." The young man nodded wordlessly, and did as instructed.

Once the three Germans were taken care of, the first man said, "Please, follow me." He led the three men through the building, which was a large, well-appointed mansion of a home in New York's Chinatown. Intricate pieces of Chinese artwork were on display throughout the home, serving as both a shrine to Chinese cultural heritage and as a display of the wealth and prestige of the home's owner.

The man led them to a conference room on the second floor, near the rear of the building. Several men were already seated within, and all but one rose and bowed when the party of Germans entered the room. Unlike his companions, that man, who sat at the far end of a long table, wore traditional Chinese robes, rather than a western business suit. He sat back in his chair, his elbows resting on the chair's arms and his fingers steepled in front of his face. His eyes narrowed as he appraised the three Germans.

"Why should we help you?" Chen Chang asked without preamble.

One of Donner's lieutenants stepped forward, his heels clicking together as he bowed. "Our interests align, honored sir," he said, his English heavily accented but understandable.

"In what way?" Chen pressed. "What do you offer that I do not already possess? Men? Weapons? I have these."

"We can eliminate," Donner interjected, irritated, "these so-called 'superheroes.' They are a thorn in both our sides, *ja?*"

"Indeed they are," Chen agreed, smiling. "What did you have in mind?"

— § —

John "Steel" Sterling walked into the bar. He kept his posture aggressive, and glared at anyone who so much as glanced in his direction. He wore elaborate makeup to disguise himself, as he was operating undercover to gather information to help his investigation with Officer Clancy into the whereabouts of Donner and his fugitive army of Nazis. His clothes were rumpled, well-worn, and of questionable quality. His hair was disheveled after he had removed his knit wool cap, and he tried only halfheartedly to fix it, as it only served to aid in his disguise.

Sterling dropped onto one of the wooden stools at the bar. He looked around; the place was dark, dirty, and seedy. At least two of the patrons he recognized from wanted posters on the walls of the police department. This was exactly the kind of dive he needed. The bartender walked over, polishing a glass with a white hand towel. He set the glass down on the bar across from Sterling and slung the towel over his shoulder.

"What'll it be, pal?" the bartender asked.

"Gimme a beer," Sterling replied sourly.

The bartender rolled his eyes. "What *kind* of beer?" he asked, exasperated.

"Do I look like I give a damn?" Sterling growled. "Cold, wet, and cheap." The bartender nodded, grabbed the glass, and turned. He slipped the glass under one of the taps nearby, pulled the handle, and filled it. Under his practiced hand, there was a modest but not overly large head, and he placed the glass in front of Sterling, who grabbed it with a nod of thanks, then turned on the stool to take in the rest of the bar and its patrons. Sipping the beer, he listened in on the conversations, his uncannily acute hearing letting him eavesdrop on what were otherwise hushed asides between the seedy patrons of the equally seedy bar.

— § —

Concealed in the shadows, the Black Cobra watched as known criminals and their associates entered and exited through the doorway. It was a sturdy, wooden door, located at the bottom of an exterior stairway that sank into the ground adjacent to a tattered old building. Paint flaked off the brick walls and metal railings. There were only a few small windows to the basement rooms behind the door, and they were frosted over from frozen condensation where they weren't blocked outright by snowdrifts.

Nearly all of the people coming and going were traveling in twos or threes. One man, however, was walking alone, and he was headed toward the alley where the Black Cobra was laying in wait. He was a large man, with tattered clothing that looked like it barely provided any protection from the cold and a dark wool cap pulled down tightly over his head. He looked to be some kind of laborer, possibly a dock worker. There was a good chance he would have the information that the Black Cobra was looking for.

The large man, his breath puffing as he walked, his hands buried in the pockets of his jacket and his head and shoulders hunched over, set against the cold, stepped where the Black Cobra had anticipated, and he sprung his trap. With the tug of a cord, a rope leaped up from beneath the snow, ensnaring the large man's feet as a lasso tightened around his ankles. The man was suddenly pulled off of his feet, and he fell forward. His hands flew out to protect himself from the fall, but it never came. His face missed the ground by inches, and he rocketed, feet-first, into the air. He came to an abrupt halt near the roof, several stories up, and began to twist.

The Black Cobra leaned forward into the light and with menace in his voice, growled, "Where are the Germans?" Incredibly, the man began to laugh.

"You goddamned idiot," he said to the Black Cobra. He glanced at the ground. No one was around when the Black Cobra had sprung his trap. Suddenly, the large man began to right himself in midair. Whoever it was the Black Cobra had caught, he could *fly*.

The man reached toward his feet, untangling them from the rope. He straightened, upright, his back to the Black Cobra, who remained motionless in his shock. The man dropped the lasso end of the rope, which began to sway from the pulley system that had brought him to the roof. He began to turn, and pulled the wool cap free from his head. His blond hair was mussed and rumpled. The Black Cobra's eyes widened, the whites large and in stark contrast to the black of his costume and the dark makeup around his eyes.

"Steel Sterling," he said softly in recognition. *"Crap."*

Sterling settled onto the roof beside the Black Cobra. "Crap, indeed," Sterling said mildly. "It seems we're heading for the same goal, though my methods are both more subtle and... well, less legally questionable. Should we compare notes?"

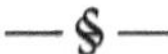

"That went well, *mein Herr*," Donner's senior lieutenant said in German after they had settled into the seats in the rear of their car. Donner glowered at the man.

"Those oriental *schwein* will betray us," Donner spat, "at their first opportunity. It is in their nature. See to it that they do not get that opportunity."

"Jawohl, mein Herr," the man replied, nodding his head.

"And once they have served their purpose," Donner continued, "we will rid ourselves of them. Permanently, I hope. The world will be better off without them." The hypocrisy of his words apparently escaped not only his notice, but also that of his lieutenants. "How go our recruiting efforts?" Donner asked.

"Better than expected, *mein Herr*," the other of Donner's lieutenants said. "There was already a well-established network of individuals who share our views on racial purity."

"Indeed," Donner said, straightening slightly, his eyebrows quirking upward in curiousity.

"Ja," the lieutenant continued. "This... Ku Klux Klan has a particular hatred for the negro, and wishes it removed. We have seized upon this to bring them to our cause."

"Excellent," Donner praised the man. "And what of our efforts to suborn the city's criminal element?"

"Less than successful, I'm afraid," the lieutenant said. "The Chinese aside, the other criminal organizations have rebuffed our advances. Though Italy was an ally of the Reich during the war, the same cannot be said of the Italian mafia in America."

"A shame," Donner replied. "Their reputation is formidable."

"We are also beginning," the lieutenant continued, "to canvass establishments known to cater to the criminal element. With luck, we may even find more superhumans to bring to our cause."

— § —

"They will betray us," one of the men in western business suits said to Chen Chang in Mandarin. "They're *Nazis*."

"And until then," Chen said, his voice low and patient, "they will take care of this 'superhero' problem for us. We will prepare for their inevitable betrayal. Once the 'heroes' have been eliminated, we will do the same to these Nazis."

"They are recruiting," another man said. "They have already formed ties with the Ku Klux Klan."

"All the better," Chen said, surprising the other men in the room. "We can be rid of those bigots as well. Two birds with one stone, as the saying goes." He paused, collecting his thoughts. "For now, we help them. At the same time, we will begin recruiting our own superhumans. I am certain they are out there; the superhuman population is beginning to explode around the world, and the Chinese population is no exception. When the time comes, we will have a force to counter this 'Donner,' and if he should fail, they can counter the 'heroes' instead."

The man nodded, practically bowing in his seat. "It will be done," he replied.

— § —

Saturday, February 20, 1954

Nucleus and Strongman stood in the large room at the van Norton estate where the small crowd of heroes was gathering. Once Steel Sterling had spoken to Strongman over the phone about what he and the Black Cobra had uncovered, Strongman began to reach out to the other heroes, and arranged for everyone to meet at his home. Along with Nucleus, he had been joined by Sterling, the Black Cobra, and Mayor Richard Wagner. The door to the room opened once again, and a man in a gray suit with bright red hair was led through the door by one of the stewards. He made his way to Strongman.

"Mr. Mayor," Strongman said, "allow me to introduce Special Agent Joe Higgins of the FBI. Agent Higgins, this is Mayor Richard Wagner." The two men smiled and shook hands.

"Given the seriousness of this matter," Higgins said, "I took the liberty of inviting one more person." Strongman cocked an eyebrow. "He should be right behind me." As if on cue, the door opened once more, and a man in an Army officer's dress uniform stepped through.

"Captain Wright!" Strongman said, smiling. He extended a hand as the Army captain stepped over to join him with Higgins, Nucleus, and the mayor.

"Van Norton," Wright said in greeting, taking Strongman's hand. "Or, should I say, *Strongman*." He turned his attention to the others. "Nucleus, Agent Higgins. Good to see you gentlemen again."

"Again?" Mayor Wagner asked. "I take it you've met everyone before, then."

"Mr. Mayor," Strongman began, "this is Captain Don Wright, U.S. Army. Captain, Mayor Richard Wagner." Wright and Wagner exchanged handshakes.

"That's quite a grip you've got, captain," Wagner remarked, wincing slightly.

Wright smiled. "I had the honor of serving with Agent Higgins, Nucleus, and Strongman during the war," he said.

"The honor was ours, sir," Strongman said, then addressed the mayor. "He was our commanding officer."

"You may have heard of Team Liberty," Wright said, grinning. "They call me Captain Freedom." Mayor Wagner's eyes bulged, and his jaw dropped slightly.

"And Higgins here was the Shield," Strongman chuckled, poking the federal agent in the side with an elbow, "before he became the g-man extraordinaire." Higgins shot him an annoyed glance.

"The Department of Defense," Wright said, interrupting the playful banter before it could continue further, "is very concerned about this situation. The brass is viewing this as an invasion of U.S. soil, and justifiably so. They're authorizing Team Liberty to deploy to counter this threat. As the commanding officer of Team Liberty, I want to work with local authorities to make sure we handle this right. In my view, that includes the local superheroes."

"What did you have in mind?" Mayor Wagner asked.

"Team Liberty," Wright said, "will deploy in a support role. Local law enforcement and your superheroes will take point. You know the lay of the land better than we do: the places, the people. We'll rely on you to find the enemy. Once we know where they are, point us in their direction, and we will annihilate them."

"We want in when you do," Nucleus said. "These bastards attacked our home. This is personal."

Chapter Seventeen
Thursday, March 4, 1954

Donner entered the office he had been using in the building that his advance forces had secured. He found two men waiting for him inside. Both were tall, thin, and had light complexions. One he recognized; the other was a stranger to him.

The man he knew had mousy brown hair. During the war, he had been a vital intelligence source in the American weapons industry, and had been given the code name "Count Berlin" by the American intelligence services, which had never managed to capture, much less identify, him. This man, who Donner knew to be John Weber, an influential weapons manufacturer, had been born Johann Weber before his parents immigrated to the United States during the Depression between the World Wars. His loyalty had secretly remained to the land of his birth, which had been his home well into his teenage years. After the war, Weber began clandestinely providing weapons to several enclaves of Nazi expatriates, including Donner's, and that contact had helped open up the doors for Donner's plans. The man with Weber had jet black hair and piercing blue eyes, and a well-manicured black goatee. Both men rose as Donner entered the room.

"Thank you," Weber began in English, extending his hand to Donner, "for agreeing to this meeting." Donner took Weber's hand and shook it.

"Without you," Donner replied in English, his accent thick but understandable for his guests, "none of this would have been possible."

"I would like you," Weber said, "to meet one of my associates. His name is Dr. Conrad Krueger, and he is an exceptionally gifted scientist. He specializes in both weapons and defensive body armor. He also has quite a bit of experience dealing with superheroes; they know him as the Black Knight."

Donner's eyebrows raised, his curiousity piqued. "Do you," he asked, "have powers as well, *Herr Doktor?*"

"Not to my knowledge," Krueger replied, "but I have fought Steel Sterling on several occasions. He has foiled several of my plans," at this Krueger growled. "But there are many others of which he knows nothing."

"Our goals," Weber interjected, "and Dr. Kruger's align quite nicely. I believe we may very easily come to a mutually-beneficial agreement."

"I have men," Krueger supplied, "facilities, weapons, and materiel. You want to rebuild the Reich. I want to be at the top with you."

Donner smiled. "I think that can be arranged," he said.

— § —

Percy van Norton and Alex Stevens got out of the car after van Norton had parked it near the building, and Stevens looked around. Though he had visited Staten Island many times before, he had never been to Fort Wadsworth; it seemed much like other military bases that he'd been to in the past. There was an order to things on a military base that, he had to admit, a part of him had missed over the last few months since he and van Norton had returned to New York. The two men entered the nondescript administrative building, and were greeted by Captain Wright.

"Welcome to Fort Wadsworth, gentlemen," Wright began, extending his arm to shake hands with the two heroes. "Thank you for coming down."

"Thanks for having us, sir," Stevens said.

"Any news on Donner?" Wright asked, leading them down the hallway.

"Not yet," van Norton replied. "Black Cobra and Steel Sterling are working on that now. Sterling has a lead that Donner is recruiting more superhumans. Black Cobra says the Chinese mob is working with him, too... and so is the Klan."

"Damn," Wright said. "We need to nip this in the bud." He opened a doorway, behind which was a concealed elevator. The heroes exchanged surprised glances as Wright stepped inside, then they followed wright into the elevator, which was little more than a steel cage built into a closet. Wright pulled the door closed, then shut a folding lattice screen door. A dim light bulb provided the only illumination. Wright pressed the sole button, and the elevator jolted, then began to descend.

"Sorry I couldn't tell you about that," Wright apologized. "Your security clearances are still valid, but operational security limits what I could disclose in public." Several moments passed before the elevator stopped at the bottom. More lights illuminated a long hallway. "This was built," Wright explained, "as a shelter for VIPs in case of nuclear attack, now that the Russians have the bomb. For the time being, Team Liberty will operate out of this facility, to maintain secrecy regarding our presence." Wright led van Norton and Stevens into the hallway. "Welcome to the Bunker."

The trio passed through the doorless hallway for a good twenty yards from the elevator's exit. It was a perfect kill zone for any hostiles that might attempt a forced entry, with no hiding places available for cover. At the end opposite the elevator, a reinforced guard shack mounted an M2 Browning .50 caliber machine gun. Overkill, perhaps, but if a facility like this was ever needed for its indended purpose, the world would certainly be in a desperate state of affairs. Two men stood inside the guard shack, peering through the slit formed between the plates of armor.

"Halt and be identified," one of the guards said as the trio came within the final five yards of the hallway. Wright stopped, and Stevens and van Norton followed suit.

"Captain Donald Wright," the officer announced. "I have two guests with me, identities classified."

"Erstwhile zeppelin," the guard said.

"Trustable bundle," Wright replied, giving the countersign. The guard on the left stepped out through a doorway behind the barrier. He emerged from the door beside the barrier, and held it open, rendering a sharp salute. His uniform was immaculate, with Staff Sergeant stripes on his sleeves and a gleaming steel pot helmet on his head.

"Welcome back, sir," the sergeant said.

"Thank you, sergeant," Wright replied, returning the salute. He stepped through the opened door, and was followed by Stevens and van Norton. The guard closed the door with a loud "click" almost as soon as they were through.

The group found themselves in a small room with halls leading away in three directions; along the fourth wall, to their right, there was a desk with another man in a sergeant's uniform. He had three ID badges waiting on the desk. Taking the badges, they pinned them to their chests. Captain Wright's featured his name and photo, while the other two simply said "visitor" in large, bold letters.

Wright led them to another elevator, next to one of the hallways, on the wall opposite the door they had entered. They waited a few moments after Wright pressed the call button. The doors opened to a typical-looking elevator, and they stepped inside.

Wright pressed the button labeled "5," and Stevens and van Norton both noticed that the numbers, unlike most elevators, got larger as they went *down*, and there were quite a few of them. Wright caught their surprised glances.

"The Bunker," Wright explained as the elevator began a smooth descent, "is designed to be self-sufficient for extended periods. Years, if necessary. Since it was designed with VIPs in mind, it has all the comforts of home: gyms, offices, a fully-stocked dining facility, even a movie theater." The elevator slowed to a stop, and the doors opened. "This is the office level," Wright said, stepping out. "This way."

Wright led them down a maze of hallways. In addition to the doorways and windows leading into offices, window-sized panels of frosted glass lined the walls of several hallways, and were lit from behind. Some of those featured shadows from cutouts shaped like tree branches, providing an illusion of being above ground, rather than the reality of being hundreds of feet beneath it.

The three men eventually entered a large room with an equally large, rectangular table that dominated the room's center. Seated around the table were almost a dozen men in uniforms from every branch of the military, many of whom Stevens and van Norton recognized. Along the far wall, at the head of the table, a map of New York City and the surrounding area was littered with pushpins. Most of those were near the docks in Manhattan, where both Strongman and Steel Sterling had visited, as well as the location of Donner's assaults on both Manhattan and the van Norton estate in the Bronx.

As Stevens and van Norton exchanged silent greetings with old friends and took a pair of empty seats near the door, Wright walked over to the head of the table. He was about to begin speaking, but stopped himself, a confused look on his face. As if on cue, Special Agent Joe Higgins, also wearing a "visitor" badge, walked into the room. Taking a seat near Stevens and van Norton, he muttered, "I hate you two."

As they looked at him, then one another, then back to him in confusion, Captain Wright asked, "Is everything all right, Agent Higgins?"

Higgins' expression soured. "I just got off the phone with Director Hoover," he said. "He's sending a package for me. When all this goes down..." His lip curled in disgust. "He wants me to wear a *costume*, captain. Like these two." He waved a hand at Stevens and van Norton. Laughter erupted around the table. Wright, who couldn't help but join in, waved it down after a moment.

"We're going to coordinate from here," Wright said, bringing the meeting back to order. "All intel on Donner and his associates will come to us, and be shared with the civilian authorities. Once his location and the strength of his forces has been determined, we will form a plan of attack and take him down for good."

— § —

"We're looking," the man in the dark overcoat said, his arms clasped behind his back, "for men with certain... *talents*." He eyed the group of men in front of him appraisingly. John "Steel" Sterling crossed his arms in front of his chest. He was in his dock worker disguise once again. He continued to listen as the man spoke. He and the others with him had been among those "recruited" at one of the many dive bars that Sterling had been frequenting in his ongoing investigation into Donner's whereabouts. When he'd heard that Donner was recruiting superhumans, he let it be known that he had "certain talents," as the man in the overcoat had just put it. It didn't take long for someone to approach him, giving him a time and an address.

Officer Clancy and his superiors in the police department hadn't been thrilled with the idea of Sterling taking on a risk like this, but he was the closest thing they had to having a superhuman on the police force, and Nucleus and Strongman were too high-profile to get away with it. So here he was, waiting to try out for the new, super-powered *Waffen-SS.*

He stepped forward when his turn came, to a man in a dark shirt and trousers seated at a folding field desk. He had a stack of papers on his left and right. As Sterling approached, he pulled one from the larger, neater stack and set it directly in front of him, between the two stacks. Sterling could see now that the shorter stack of papers had writing on it, and the papers were all forms. He'd heard that the Germans were notorious for their meticulous paperwork; now he was seeing it for himself.

"Name?" the man at the field desk asked.

"Johnson," Sterling lied. "John Johnson."

The man repeated the name in a thick German accent as he wrote on the form, and it sounded more like "Yon Yons-sohn." He finished writing, then asked, "Age?"

"Twenty-two," Sterling said.

The German repeated in his heavy accent, then noted on his own, *"Blonde haar, blaue augen... gut, sehr gut."* The questions continued for several minutes, and when they had reached the end of the form, the German man directed Sterling to wait with a group of men to one side of the room.

Once the entire group had been interviewed, another man came into the room. He read through the forms, and set aside several into a separate pile. The German who had been conducting the interviews took the small sheaf of forms that the other man had selected, then addressed the group. He read several names, and Sterling took a moment to register that his alias had been among them. After reading the names, the man said, "Gentlemen, please follow my associate." He raised an arm, indicating the other man, who was already heading for the door he had entered just minutes earlier. Sterling began to follow, and the phrase "down the rabbit hole" came, unbidden, to mind.

— § —

"Nobody move, and nobody gets hurt!" shouted a giant of a man leading a group of four other men into the bank lobby. All wore face-concealing ski masks, and all were heavily armed. They dispersed into the bank, fanning through the large, marbled lobby. The lead bank robber threw a cloth sack at the nearest teller. "Fill this up," he ordered. Eyes wide, she set to work as he leveled a Tommy gun in her direction.

Suddenly, a cloud of dark smoke billowed up near the bank entrance. Then another. And another. Indistinct forms moved quickly through the smoke. With the sound of shattered glass, the lights began to go out, one by one, in quick succession. As the bank robbers' eyes attempted to adjust to the sudden change in light, shadowy forms grabbed them, and the sounds of brief struggles could be heard throughout the lobby.

A foot shot out of the darkness toward the hulking lead bank robber. He blocked it, having realized what was happening: two heroes, probably the Black Cobra and the Arrow, were here, and they had already taken out the other four men with him. But he had a surprise up his sleeve.

The huge man put his fists up in front of his chest, arms relaxed and ready to strike. He listened, relying more on his ears than his limited sight. Hearing the light scuff of a booted foot on the marble floor, he pivoted, and launched an arm in an uppercut. He made contact with something solid, and heard a crash as whatever he'd hit went flying.

— § —

The Black Cobra blinked as he picked himself back up. There had been no problem taking down the other four bank robbers, but their leader was in a different class altogether. For a single punch to send him flying like that, it could only mean one thing: this man was a superhuman. He may not be on the same level as Strongman or Steel Sterling, but he was still far stronger than a normal man, and the Black Cobra needed to adjust his tactics accordingly.

The bank robber was a brute of a man, and had to be seven or even eight feet tall. As he began to stalk toward the Black Cobra, a fusillade of arrows clattered against the floor, bouncing off the polished marble.

The man paused briefly, glancing in the direction where the arrows had come from, and shot a glare at the Arrow, whose bow was still at the ready and pointed in his direction. He turned his attention back to the Black Cobra, and continued his slow, menacing advance.

The Black Cobra raised his fists into a fighting stance. As he steeled himself for a hard fight, more arrows came flying. One ripped into the bank robber's calf, and he bellowed in pain. *So*, the Black Cobra thought, *at least he's not invulnerable.* Clearly emboldened by the success, the Arrow sent more arrows into the hide of the super-strong thug. They buried themselves into his arm, leg, and shoulder. The thug howled in renewed agony.

"Surrender," the Black Cobra urged, weaving from side to side and keeping his fists ready for a fight. "It's over. You *can't* win this one."

"The Boss don't surrender ta no one!" the man replied, pulling the arrows out of himself with easy—if pained—tugs. He threw the arrows to one side, and they clattered on the marble floor.

The Black Cobra, never taking his eyes from his opponent—who apparently called himself the Boss—reached with one hand to a pouch on his belt. Taking a deep breath, he held it and threw a pellet at the feet of the Boss. It erupted into a cloud of white smoke that quickly enveloped the giant man. The Black Cobra waited as the Boss coughed, trying to fan the smoke from obscuring his vision.

"You think that's gonna stop me?" the Boss asked between coughs. "I don't… I don't need ta… I don't…" With a thundering crash, the brute fell, face-first, into a check-writing table, which was immediately reduced to splinters. His eyes were closed, and a thin puddle of drool began to collect underneath his mouth.

The Arrow joined the Black Cobra, having vacated his perch moments after the Boss collapsed into unconsciousness. He slung his bow over his shoulder. "Knockout gas," the Arrow commented. "Nice."

"At least I didn't put a half-dozen holes in him," the Black Cobra replied bitterly. "You're really pushing Nucleus' edict not to use lethal force."

"He's naive," the Arrow replied dismissively.

"He's anything *but*," the Black Cobra said. He bent down and began to tie the Boss' hands behind his back. Then he thought a moment, and bound his arms as well. Even then, he wasn't sure if it would be enough to secure him. "He knows the law, and his limits under it."

The Arrow scoffed. "The law," he said derisively, "doesn't do anything to stop the rich and powerful from doing whatever they want."

"We have to work within the law," the Black Cobra replied evenly, "or we're no better than the thugs we just stopped. Now go tie them up so they don't cause trouble when they wake up again."

Sterling followed the group into another room. Inside, to his surprise, Donner himself was waiting for them, sitting on the edge of a desk. He tensed, and tried to force himself to relax. He was disguised, and no one had recognized him so far, but Donner was a different story. He had been *inches* away from him when they had fought a few weeks ago.

"Thank you for coming, gentlemen," Donner said in a thick German accent. "You have been chosen to help us take down the corrupt system here in America, starting with New York City. You have powers, like me. *We* are the future."

"You're Donner," one of the other men said in shock. "I saw you on the news. You're a damned *Nazi!*" He turned for the door. "I ain't workin' for no Nazis!" A bolt of lightning shot from Donner's hand, immediately striking the man in the back. He crumpled to the floor, thick black smoke emanating from a patch of charred fabric on the back of his coat. Donner hadn't even moved.

"No," Donner said. "You are not." He stood and approached the other men in the group. "Would anyone else care to leave?"

Chapter Eighteen
Friday, March 5, 1954

Two men stood before Donner's desk. They, like Donner, wore nondescript clothing. One of the two men was extremely young, perhaps barely having reached his eighteenth birthday. The man standing beside him was at least twice his age; he had been a young *Unteroffizer*—a junior noncommissioned officer rank in the *Wehrmacht*—at the end of the war, and he was once again a noncommissioned officer for Donner's army a decade later. Donner nodded for them to report their news.

"Mein Herr," the older man said, reflexively coming to attention as he spoke. *"Stabsscharführer* Hörst," he introduced himself. His new rank was that of a senior non-commissioned officer in the *Waffen-SS*, comparable to a company-level sergeant major in the United States Army.

"Hörst?" Donner asked, interrupting the man. "Any relation to General Viktor Hörst?"

"My father," the senior NCO replied. "I understand that he was a friend of *your* father."

"Did he survive the war?" Donner asked. "I last saw him in Berlin."

"No, *mein Herr,*" Hörst replied, his eyes casting to the floor momentarily. "He arranged for me to escort my mother and sisters to safety, but could not join us. He was captured and executed by the Allies."

"You have my condolences," Donner said. After a moment, he asked, "Now, what do you have for me, *Spieß?*" The use of the nickname for Hörst's position caused his mood to brighten slightly.

"This young man," Hörst replied, "*Schütze Georg* Schreiber." The rank was the equivalent of a private. "He has begun to display... abilities." Donner's eyes brightened.

"What *sort of abilities?*" Donner asked.

"He," Hörst began uncertainly, then interrupted himself. "*Mein Herr,* I believe it would be easier if you saw it for yourself." Donner nodded, and Hörst prompted, "When you are ready, *Schütze.*"

Schreiber nodded. He bent over slightly, and removed his shoes. Donner leaned to peer over his desk, but saw nothing unusual about the young man's feet. Setting the shoes neatly to the side, Schreiber stepped over to one of the walls. He placed his hands tentatively on the smooth wall, then lifted his right leg, placing his sock-covered foot on the wall. He pushed up with that leg... and began to *climb.* Donner applauded with unbridled glee.

"Excellent!" he cheered. Schreiber reached the top of the wall, then began to crawl across the ceiling. Donner redoubled his applause, smiling broadly. Schreiber stopped midway across the ceiling, near where Hörst still stood. He released his grip, then spun and flipped in midair, landing perfectly on his feet, back where he'd started.

"Amazing," Donner said. "Spectacular." He paused a moment, then continued, "I am transferring you to my special *übermensch* division. As you are also the only other German übermensch at present, I am placing you in command, unless another, more senior German soldat develops powers as well. To that end, I am also promoting you. Congratulations, *Untersturmführer* Schreiber." Donner rose and extended his hand, unable to stop smiling broadly.

— § —

"This is *Untersturmführer* Schreiber," the tall, thin German man standing next to Schreiber said in a thick accent, addressing the group of American superhuman recruits. "He is still learning English, so I will serve as his translator. I am *Scharführer* Schmidt."

"What's all this '*führer*' stuff?" somebody called out in a thick Brooklyn accent.

Schmidt sighed. "The word *'führer'* just means 'leader,'" he explained. "*Untersturmführer* and *Scharführer* are ranks. There is not a precise translation, but in your terms, an *Untersturmführer* is like a *Leutnant,*" he pronounced the rank "lieutenant" like its German army equivalent, "and a *Scharführer* is like a sergeant." Schreiber and Schmidt exchanged a brief dialogue in rushed German. When they were finished speaking, Schmidt returned his attention to the recruits. Within the group of recruits, Steel Sterling, operating undercover as a super-powered dock worker named John Johnson, listened intently.

"We are here," Schmidt said, "to train you to work as part of a team. It is my hope that you learn fast, because we already have a job for you."

— $ —

Friday, March 12, 1954

Alex Stevens and Percy van Norton exited the gymnasium on the fourth level of the Bunker with a group of their old friends from their days in Team Liberty. Everyone was laughing and trading stories about the things that had happened in their lives over the past year, following the end of the Korean War in July and the end of Stevens and van Norton's enlistments in November.

"So then," van Norton said, laughing, "he comes to me and says, 'They thought I was a bad guy.'" The rest of the group erupted in renewed laughter. "He was trying to fight crime in a ski mask, and he was *surprised* that people thought he was a bad guy!" Stevens, though mildly embarrassed, joined in on the laughter. He had to admit, it was pretty funny.

As the group made their way to the locker room, the speakers mounted throughout the facility crackled to life. "All Team Liberty personnel," a tinny voice said, "and guests Stevens and van Norton, report to the briefing room in twenty minutes. I say again, all Team Liberty personnel and guests Stevens and van Norton, report to the briefing room in twenty minutes." There was a hiss of static followed by a click a moment later, and the speakers went silent again. Everyone in the group looked at one another, shrugged, and headed for the showers.

Twenty minutes later, everyone gathered, freshly showered and changed, in the briefing room. While there were several faces that they knew, half of the team had joined after Stevens and van Norton had left. With Stevens and van Norton were old friends: Navy petty officers Jason "Mimic" Ochoa and Chuck "Samson" Hardy and Seaman Tom "Typhoon" Sanders, Air Force Senior Airman Ray "Firebrand" O'Reilly, and Army Corporal Fred "Lightning" Larkin. Opposite them at the briefing room table were the newer members of the team, who Stevens and van Norton were still getting to know: Marine Lance Corporal Jim "Dynamo" Andrews and Private First Class Joe "Grendel" Myers; Army Private First Class Duke "Meteor" O'Dowd, Corporal Bill "Gargoyle" Moore, and Sergeant Rick "Eagle" Perez; and finally Navy Able Seaman Danny "Luckyman" Barr. At the head of the briefing room table, Captain Don Wright, *aka* Captain Freedom, and FBI Special Agent Joe "The Shield" Higgins stood in front of a map of New York City.

Mimic was one of the first people that Stevens and van Norton met after they had arrived at Fort Leonard Wood, more than a year earlier. Jason Ochoa was an otherwise unassuming-looking hispanic man from southern California. He had joined the Navy prior to the start of the Korean War. When his ship was struck by enemy artillery fire from the coast, his life was saved when his body transformed into the same steel as the ship's hull. His crewmates in his section, sadly, were not so fortunate. Samson, like Strongman, was gifted with super-strength and invulnerability; perhaps fittingly, Chuck Hardy was a large, powerfully-built black man from Chicago.

Firebrand's bright red hair served as a perfect match to his flame-based powers. Although Ray O'Reilly couldn't fly like their former teammate Jack Knapp, who'd earned the obvious nickname Blue Flame, O'Reilly, who hailed from Toledo, Ohio, could create and manipulate flames, which had saved not only his life, but the lives of everyone aboard the C-47 Skytrain cargo plane, known affectionately as a "Gooneybird," that he was serving aboard as a loadmaster when its engines caught fire.

Typhoon could breathe underwater, a fact that Tom Sanders discovered when an accident caused his ship to start taking on water while he was trapped below decks. When a recovery team was sent in, expecting to find a drowned body, they instead found him alive and well, despite having spent several hours submerged in freezing waters.

Lightning was the last of the original members of Team Liberty. Fred Larkin discovered his powers after being struck by lightning while on patrol in Korea during a thunderstorm. Not only did he survive the strike without so much as a scratch, he soon discovered that he could control electrical currents and generate lighting bolts of his own. He couldn't fly like Donner, so far as he knew, but his powers were otherwise similar.

Dynamo was one of the new additions to the team; Jim Andrews didn't have as dramatic a story as Lightning, but they shared similar electrical-based powers. Grendel, whose name came from the monster in the epic poem *Beowulf*, discovered his powers during an ambush by North Korean forces. Joe Myers, pinned down by an overwhelming enemy force, suddenly transformed into a hulking monstrosity that singlehandedly wiped out an entire North Korean company.

Gargoyle had a similar story, but when Bill Moore's body turned to stone, it didn't turn back to normal after the threat had passed. Meteor got his name from his ability to fly, but it turned out that Duke O'Dowd actually had magnetism-based powers, and he flew in much the same way as Steel Sterling, by repelling himself from the Earth's molten metal core. Eagle could also fly, but so far, Ricardo "Rick" Perez hadn't shown any other abilities. Luckyman earned his name from having luck turn out to be his power. The scientists called it "involuntary localized probability control," but it boiled down to the same thing: everything always went Danny Barr's way. Always.

"We've received word from the mayor's office," Agent Higgins began, "that Steel Sterling has made contact. He has successfully infiltrated Donner's forces, and has given us their location." Everyone exchanged glances. "He has provided an impressive level of actionable intelligence, including estimated force strengths, alliances with local organizations, and even details of an upcoming operation."

"This is our opportunity," Captain Wright said, "to engage and defeat the enemy. Donner is expecting a new shipment of weapons tomorrow, which is being smuggled in through the ports once again. He knows that we are watching the ports, and is personally leading a force of superhuman recruits, SS soldiers, and Ku Klux Klansmen to safeguard the extraction of the shipment.

"We will split into two squads," Wright continued. "I will lead Able Squad, which will intercept and engage Donner and his forces at the docks. The Shield will lead Baker Squad, which will assault Donner's base of operations in conjunction with local law enforcement. Team assignments will be posted within the hour."

— $ —

"Jesus, I look ridiculous," the Shield muttered as he looked at his reflection in the window of a police cruiser. He wore a red-white-and-blue eyesore, and the entire front of the gaudy outfit was designed to look like a *literal* shield. The majority of the outfit was red: bodysuit, cowl (which let his red hair show), and cape, with blue gloves and boots. The shield on his front had a blue rectangle with three huge, white stars on top, and a half-dozen red and white stripes at the bottom.

"It's certainly patriotic," a voice said from behind him. The Shield spun, and found the Black Cobra emerging from the shadows. "Agent Higgins, right? Or is it the Shield again?" The Black Cobra extended his hand. "I'm the Black Cobra. We met at Strongman's house."

"I remember," the Shield replied, shaking the Black Cobra's hand. "Might as well stick with 'the Shield' while I'm in this getup." He sighed. "I'm about to go introduce myself to the lead officer. Tag along if you'd like." The Shield turned and walked away.

As he approached, the Shield realized that the officer in charge here at the staging area was the Police Commissioner himself, Francis Adams. As he made his way closer to the commissioner, he could hear Adams mutter, "Aw, Christ, another one." Ignoring the comment, the Shield held out a gloved hand, and the commissioner looked at it as if it were diseased.

"Special Agent Joe Higgins, FBI," the Shield introduced himself. After a moment, he added, "The director insisted that I wear this, and yes, I feel as ridiculous as I look." He pulled his FBI credentials from a pocket on his belt, and held them up for the commissioner to inspect.

"Agent Higgins," Commissioner Adams said by way of greeting. "Do you have a ridiculous name to go with your ridiculous outfit?"

"The Shield," he said, groaning.

"It's bad," the commissioner remarked, "when even the FBI want in on this superhero nonsense."

"You're preaching to the choir," the Shield lamented. After a moment, he said, "I'm here to coordinate between the police department and Team Liberty. I'll be leading Team Liberty's Baker Squad, which will take point, just in case Donner left any superhuman surprises guarding the hen house." The commissioner shifted his weight uncomfortably. *Great,* the Shield thought.

—$—

"That's the ship," Captain Freedom said, pointing to a freighter moored at one of the docks in the port, midway along the length of the pier. "It docked this afternoon, and hasn't started unloading its cargo yet." Night was falling, and the soft glow of the street lamps was quickly becoming the brightest light source available.

"Now," Nucleus said, "we wait."

The minutes seemed to last forever. In reality, only half an hour had passed when a large group of men began to march down the pier. At the forefront, Donner was clearly visible. He was wearing an old Nazi general's uniform: his father's uniform. Behind him were dozens of men. A half-dozen wore civilian clothing. About two dozen wore Nazi uniforms like Donner. Nearly three dozen wore the white, hooded robes of the Ku Klux Klan.

"It's a trap," Strongman breathed. "They outnumber the superheroes ten to one."

"Sterling's intel was good," Captain Freedom said, grinning. He keyed the radio set up near his position. "This is Captain Freedom. All units: go."

Chapter Nineteen

John "Steel" Sterling, operating under the alias "John Johnson," marched behind *Untersturmführer* Schreiber and *Scharführer* Schmidt, who were directly behind Donner himself, as the Nazi forces marched down the pier toward the freighter carrying the supplies that Donner needed to continue carrying out his insurgent war to restore the Reich. As far as Donner was aware, the only opposition that he faced was a handful of local superheroes and the New York Police Department. The force he'd assembled, bolstering his own forces with recruits from the Ku Klux Klan, Sterling's own nemesis the Black Knight, and a handful of local superhumans with more bigotry and greed than sense, with logistical support from the Chinese mob, would certainly have been enough to counter those odds.

What Donner hadn't counted on was the U.S. military covertly bringing its own superhumans and special operations forces into the mix. Donner seemed incapable of formulating plans that didn't involve direct, open assaults, and his weakness, tactically speaking, was his inability to imagine anyone else doing so.

Sterling had managed to infiltrate Donner's operations by posing as a super-strong dock worker. His constant fear of discovery proved unfounded, however, as Donner failed to recognize him when they had met more than a week earlier. He had used one of his more subtle powers to relay information back to the police, who then relayed it to the FBI and Team Liberty: he could manipulate electromagnetic fields, including those in telephone wires, to both "hear" conversations and to send signals, and had covertly sent word back by simply grabbing hold of, or even stepping on, a telephone cord.

Behind Sterling, the other superhuman recruits followed. There were four left, with one having been killed by Donner for refusing to work for the Nazis. The remaining four hadn't stayed out of fear, but out of their own greed and desire to hurt people. Three of the four were directly behind him. Brett Hannigan was a skinny, dark-haired man who could turn himself into a werewolf-like creature whenever he wanted—not just on a full moon—and he had total control of his actions in his alternate form, unlike most of the werewolves of mythology. The skin on Xavier Exley's right hand was blackened, earning him the obvious nickname of "Black Fist," and if he touched someone with it, he could drain their life energy. Rory Weber was a stocky, barrel-chested man who also had super-strength, though not to the same degree as Sterling or Strongman. The fourth recruit, a willowy man named Julius Iles, was quickly nicknamed "the Eel," due to his slender frame and ability to breathe underwater; he was currently swimming somewhere in the area, planting explosives and waiting for his moment to strike.

Without warning, floodlights snapped on, bathing the pier in illumination. A voice called out, amplified over a loudspeaker: "Attention! This is Captain Freedom of Team Liberty. We have you surrounded. Surrender now. There is no need for hostilities."

Yeah, Sterling thought, *like that's gonna work.*

— § —

Floodlights lit up the sides of the building and the surrounding streets. There was a flurry of motion in several windows as shades were quickly drawn and people darted away from sight.

"This is the police!" Commissioner Adams' voice bellowed through a loudspeaker. "We have the building surrounded! Come out with your hands up!" Automatic weapons fire erupted from several windows, as evidenced by the muzzle flashes and hundreds of bullets impacting against the pavement, police cars, and several police officers.

"Take cover!" someone yelled as the other police officers were already diving for safety. "Officers down!" Several of the officers began to move from their own safe cover, and tried to pull their fallen brothers-in-arms to safety, where their wounds could be treated. Weapons fire burst forth from the building once again, forcing the officers back into their positions of cover, and they returned fire. Glass shattered, and screams could be heard from a neighboring building.

The concrete pavement on the pier cracked and splintered as Grendel's hulking form slammed into it, having dropped several stories up from the crane, transforming on his way to the ground. He was enormous, his muscles rippling under his dark skin; his jaw became elongated, filled with razor-sharp teeth, and his tongue snaked out to lick his growing muzzle. His nails became sharp talons, and he hunched over menacingly. Other members of Team Liberty emerged, surrounding Donner's combined force of Nazis and Ku Klux Klansmen. Strongman dropped from a nearby ship's deck, landing on the pier with enough force to rattle several nearby crates.

Samson emerged from behind a stack of crates, brandishing his Browning Automatic Rifle, known to the soldiers who carried them as, simply, a BAR. Captain Freedom soared out from the deck of the ship that Strongman had just left, and stopped, hovering several yards above and behind the enemy forces, an M1 Carbine at the ready in his hands. Nucleus emerged from the same ship's deck, and dropped to the ground several yards in front of Donner. Firebrand and Lightning appeared at the flanks of the enemy forces, and they were quickly joined by dozens of soldiers from another special operations unit, who emerged from their places of concealment throughout the pier and aboard nearby ships to bring their rifles to bear, and the Nazi forces brought their own rifles to bear at the same time. A tense silence reigned for several moments.

"I'll ask again," Captain Freedom yelled. "Surrender. We have you surrounded." In reply, Donner hurled a lightning bolt at the flying man. To Donner's shock, it never reached its target. Instead, it changed course midway, arcing back down, where it went instead into Lightning's outstretched hand.

The American forces opened fire immediately. As bullets tore into the ground around him and several of the men formed up behind him, Donner shot into the sky, and Nucleus and Captain Freedom launched themselves after him. Strongman grabbed a crate, and hurled it at the

Nazi forces. Samson hefted his BAR and began firing. The Nazis and Klansmen dove for what little cover they could find, and brought their own weapons to bear.

Hannigan began to shift into his werewolf form, and Sterling grabbed him. To the lycanthrope's utter shock, his supposed ally picked him up, hefted him over his head, and heaved him toward the water. The wolf-man was sent soaring, and landed with a splash hundreds of yards away. He sputtered, enraged, and began to swim back toward the pier.

— § —

The Shield leaped onto the wall of the building, digging his hands into the brick to pull himself up. Luckyman walked calmly into the open street, where he lifted a wounded police officer to his feet. Bullets pinged into the sides of police car doors and chips of asphalt flew into the air around their feet as they calmly made their way back to safety.

Touching a plate of metal on his belt, Mimic's skin suddenly became a reflective, silvery color. The belt featured several such plates, each with a material that offered different, tactically useful properties. Mimic rose, then stepped out into the open, joining Luckyman. Bullets ricocheted as they struck his now-steel skin, bouncing off of him without leaving so much as a scratch, though they did tear his clothing wherever they struck. Any ricochets that went in Luckyman's direction impacted anywhere but within three feet of the man. In a matter of minutes, the duo managed to retrieve every wounded police officer.

A scream drew their attention to the building. The Shield had reached one of the windows on the second floor, where a gunman was firing at the police. The Shield had grabbed the man, then pulled him out of the window. The man dropped his Kalashnikov, which clattered to the pavement. The Shield held the man for a moment by the collar, the man's feet dangling two stories above the ground, and then threw him back into the building. A loud crash announced his impact against the far wall of the room.

Another window, on the third floor, suddenly stopped firing. A moment later, gunshots sounded from within. There was the sound of furniture crashing down. With the shattering of glass, a man went flying out of the window. He arced away, only to stop, mid-arc, and rush back toward the building. He hit the brick wall with a resounding thud, then hung limply from a rope that was lassoed around his chest and hooked under his arms.

The Shield pushed his way into the window on the second floor. A few moments later, another window stopped firing on the third floor. Then another on the fourth. Someone leaned out of the fourth floor window, dropping his Kalashnikov to the pavement below. A moment later, he pitched forward out of the window as well. He plummeted toward the ground, and impacted the pavement with a wet crunch.

There was no further weapons fire from the windows, but the sound of Kalashnikovs could be heard coming from inside the building. Dynamo, Gargoyle, Mimic, and Luckyman surged forward from the police lines, and ran into the building's entrance, making their way inside as well. From above, Eagle and Meteor dove toward the building's roof, and breached their way through a locked stairwell door with a burst of fire from Eagle's rifle.

— § —

The water roiled near the site of the battle on the pier. Just below the surface, Typhoon and the Eel grappled, kicked, and punched. Neither could gain the upper hand, but Typhoon had at least stopped the Eel from setting any of the explosives he had been carrying. That bag was now settling at the bottom of the harbor, useless.

The evenly-matched opponents had lost their weapons early on during the fight, and were now relying on the most basic weapons available to them: their fists and feet. But Typhoon was quickly realizing that he had one weapon that outclassed anything the Eel had: his mind. He had far greater training in hand-to-hand combat than the Eel, and even with the conditions of fighting underwater being much different than fighting on the ground, he had an advantage there, as well: his training over the past year as a member of Team Liberty.

Typhoon feinted, and lured the Eel another foot closer to his goal. Kick. Hit. Flip. Block. Dodge. Evade. Foot by foot, Typhoon goaded the Eel closer to the end of this contest. They were close enough now that Typhoon could see the faint shadow of his target. He could only hope that the Eel would be unable to realize what he had planned, or at least have sufficient tunnel vision on the fight that he wouldn't notice his surroundings until it was too late.

His hopes were rewarded when the Eel followed his latest feint. He slugged the Eel in the jaw as hard as he could, hoping it would disorient the man long enough to spring his trap. He rocketed up, and shot onto the deck of a small boat. Landing hard on the deck, he flipped a switch, releasing a spring-loaded pulley assembly. He ducked as the pulley arm shot across the deck and lifted into the air. A net emerged from the water, and the Eel was wrapped within it, thrashing against the strands that had ensnared his limbs. He let out a howl of frustrated defeat.

— § —

Schreiber spun, his eyes wide with shock. He yelled something in German at Sterling, but the disguised hero could only guess at what he had said. Given the situation, however, it was more than likely something along the lines of, "What are you *doing?*"

Schmidt turned to say something, but Sterling would never know what that was. Right at that moment, Schmidt's jaw exploded in a spray of blood and bone fragments. He fell to the ground, a gurgled scream emanating from his destroyed mouth. Schreiber lived up to the nickname that the recruits had given him: the Creeper. Choosing the better part of valor, Schreiber turned and ran. Leaping toward a wall, he clung to its face and crawled toward the shadows, seeking concealment.

Black Fist charged Sterling. The hero wasn't sure if his invulnerability would protect him from the crazed man or not, and he didn't want to take any chances. He dodged the blow easily enough; Black Fist was left handed, and his power was concentrated in his blackened right hand. He was clumsy in his right-handed attacks, and telegraphed where his next punch was headed.

Sterling avoided another punch, then a clumsy attempt to grab his arm. He whipped an arm around, and punched Black Fist in the gut. The man doubled over, gasping for air, and Sterling was glad he'd pulled the punch. He was was no killer.

— § —

The Black Cobra dodged as the whip cracked past him, splintering the wood of a chair near where he'd been standing a moment earlier.

"You are wise to move so quickly," the man in the black SS uniform said, smiling, in a thick German accent. "I am *Scharführer* Helmut

Schulz, and during the war, I used this whip to execute many prisoners. I could kill you with a single slash!"

The Black Cobra continued to dodge, weave, and somersault throughout the room. The man was clearly quite dangerous with his weapon of choice, but he was fairly certain the man's braggadocio was laced with a goodly amount of hyperbole. Nevertheless, that whip could still do a lot of damage, even if it didn't kill him in a single blow, and he preferred not to take any hits if he could avoid it.

As he cartwheeled over a table, the Black Cobra grabbed a letter opener that lay near a pile of papers. When he landed on his feet, he spun quickly and hurled the makeshift weapon at Schulz. His aim was true, and it impaled itself deeply into the Nazi's hand. Schulz cried out in pain, dropping the whip. His left hand shot over to its wounded counterpart, and Schulz reached to remove the blade.

The Black Cobra didn't give Schulz the chance to recover, and kicked the Nazi across the jaw as quickly and as hard as he could. Schulz's head snapped to the side, and he flew several feet, landing hard on his back. Disoriented, Schulz struggled to recover and pick himself up from the floor, but the Black Cobra's boot slammed into his head once again.

Schulz slumped limply to the floor, unconscious. Breathing heavily, the Black Cobra looked around, then grabbed the discarded whip from the floor, where it had fallen several feet away. He rolled Schulz over, then began tying the man's hands and feet together with the whip.

The building's exterior now clear, Officer Clancy approached the corpse that had fallen four stories to its death. The body was that of a man in his late twenties or early thirties, and it was laying on its side, which seemed odd. Clancy tapped the body with his shoe, his revolver at the ready, and it rolled over onto its back... with an arrow sticking out of its chest.

Clancy only knew of one person running around who used arrows. He was rumored to have killed at least one person before he went public when Donner attacked. Clancy had also heard that Nucleus made it clear that the Arrow wouldn't use lethal force... but Nucleus wasn't here, and the arrow sticking out of this body's chest was pretty damning. Clancy doffed his cap and scratched his red hair while letting out a breath.

"Lieutenant," Clancy called, turning his head toward the police line, "you'd better come take a look at this."

CHAPTER TWENTY

Nucleus dodged as Donner hurled another bolt of lightning in his direction. Once again, Donner had run away the moment the fight started to turn against him, leaving his followers to pay the price. If it hadn't led to so many deaths and so much destruction already, it would have been laughable.

Donner, it was becoming clear to Nucleus, was a spoiled, petulant child. He lashed out with his powers to bully everyone into giving him whatever he wanted, but like all bullies, he folded as soon as he was faced with any serious resistance. After years of walking over anyone in his path, he was finally meeting someone who wouldn't back down, and he was throwing a tantrum about it.

Bullets whipped through the air as Captain Freedom opened fire with his M1 Carbine. Donner weaved to avoid the gunfire, and Nucleus fired a burst of plasma. Caught in the crossfire, Donner took a hit on his left shoulder, and plummeted toward the pier below.

Donner, his shoulder scorched by the plasma, hit the concrete platform like a brick, and the paved surface shattered under the force of the impact. Slowly, Donner began to pick himself up off of the ground, his entire body crying out in pain. As he rose, a pair of combat boots stopped in front of him.

"Stay down," a deep, basso voice urged. Donner laughed, bitterly. He wouldn't stay down. Electricity began to crackle between his fingers as he rose to his feet. When he stood, he stopped for a moment, blinking in confusion. He'd expected to find Captain Freedom standing over him.

"I said," Samson said evenly, clearly enunciating each word, *"stay down."* He lifted his right arm, then brought his fist down across Donner's jaw. The Nazi crumpled back to the ground under the blow. Donner lay on his side for several seconds, dazed. His vision swam, and for a moment, he saw three identical black men towering over him. They coalesced into a single individual, and Donner called down a bolt of lightning from the heavens to smite the impudent man for daring to strike his betters.

The lightning hit Samson squarely in the chest, and the air reeked of ozone from the blast. Donner was blinded by the flash of light for a moment. When his vision returned, he saw Samson. The black soldier was still standing, utterly unmoved by the lightning bolt. Indeed, if anything, it had only served to irritate him. He racked the slide on the BAR in his hands, pointed the barrel of the weapon directly at Donner's head, and scowled.

"Don't," he said between gritted teeth, "move."

— § - —

The Shield made his way from the room where he'd entered the building into the hallway, after having first checked, then bound, the man he'd incapacitated on his way in. A gunshot rang out, a deafening roar that reverberated off of the walls, and a bullet caromed off of his invulnerable right cheek, burying itself in the wall nearby. The Shield turned his head and looked down the hall in the direction that the gunshot had come from. A man lowered his pistol, the barrel still smoking. His eyes were so wide, they were practically circles of white surrounding the dark irises, and the color was rapidly draining from the man's face.

He ran back into a room on the opposite side of the hallway from the doorway that the Shield had just exited, and slammed the door behind him. The lock clicked into place, and the Shield nearly laughed. He stepped down the hallway, took the door handle in his hand, and turned the knob. Metal screeched and crunched as brute strength overpowered and obliterated the locking mechanism. With a tap, he swung the door open, then, on a lark, rapped on the door frame with a knuckle.

"FBI," he announced. He saw three men standing in the room opposite the door, staring in petrified horror. Something slammed into the left side of his jaw with a clang, and his head snapped to the right.

Looking down, he saw a disc-shaped, metal shield had bounced off of his face, landing on the floor in front of him. He looked in surprise as what was, for all intents and purposes, Captain America's shield lay bouncing and spinning at his feet, except it was solid red rather than striped, and in the white circle at its center was a black swastika. *Oh, now that's just wrong*, the Shield thought as a blond-haired, blue-eyed Nazi *übermensch* punched him in the head.

— § - —

Sturmmann Günter Diefenbach took cover behind a crate. This was not going well. They had been assured that they would face, at most, three or four American *übermenschen*, and perhaps a dozen or more police officers. Instead, they were pinned down, and their force of a half-dozen *übermenschen* had been utterly decimated in the battle's opening moments, along with the two dozen *Waffen-SS* soldaten and three dozen Ku Klux Klansmen, by at least six American *übermenschen* and dozens of soldiers. The pier had become a death trap, when they had been promised a cake walk.

Diefenbach checked the ammunition in his Kalashnikov. Though the rifle was Russian-made, it reminded him strongly of the *Sturmgewehr* 44 rifles he'd seen as a child during the war. The fact that the Soviets needed to copy the design so closely served only to reaffirm German superiority in his mind. Reassured that he had plenty of ammunition, he closed his eyes, took a deep breath, and offered a silent prayer.

Diefenbach turned and stood just high enough to see over the mid-sized crate, using the rest of its bulk as cover from incoming American weapons fire. He knew it was far from adequate cover, particularly from the soldiers on the decks of the ships above him, but it was still better than being out in the open. The angle made it all but impossible to get a clean shot on the impromptu snipers, but he could at least keep them pinned down and unable to effectively fire on his own forces.

Bullets ricocheted loudly off of the steel plates of the ships, and Diefenbach was rewarded with the sight of the American soldiers diving for cover, away from their own shooting positions. Several of his fellow *soldaten* were beginning to do the same, and the sound of gunfire was no longer coming almost exclusively from above.

Dynamo, Gargoyle, Luckyman, and Mimic breached the door of the building with a single blow from Gargoyle's stone-like fist. Luckyman led the way in; any enemy fire would hit anything but him or anyone standing directly behind him, thanks to his ability to subtly influence probability in his vicinity.

Dynamo followed closely behind Luckyman, while Mimic and Gargoyle took up rear guard positions. Gargoyle's skin, while not completely impervious to gunfire, was nevertheless extraordinarily resilient, and Mimic had maintained his own invulnerability by copying the steel plate bolted onto the special belt that he wore.

The squad of super-powered soldiers kept their weapons at the ready. While he wore an M1911 .45-caliber semi-automatic pistol in a holster on his hip, Dynamo instead held his hands in fists at waist level, and they crackled with electricity. The others all had, in addition to pistols of their own, rifles of different types. Luckyman carried an M1 Carbine and a backpack loaded with equipment, his finger safely off—but near—the trigger, the barrel pointed at the floor; even with his uncanny luck, he didn't want to risk an accidental discharge, and weapons safety had been drilled into him long before his powers had emerged. Mimic carried an M1 Garand, and Gargoyle served as the squad's heavy weapons operator, effortlessly carrying a BAR.

They entered a large room filled with tables and chairs, which appeared to be a makeshift cafeteria. On the opposite side of the room, two men stood, wearing black SS uniforms. Oddly, they bore no weapons. One was tall, so thin that he was practically gaunt, and he had black hair and a pencil-thin black moustache. His companion was relatively short and thickly muscled, with curly blond hair. Electricity crackled around his clenched fists. The squad recognized the men from their briefings on the intelligence sent by Steel Sterling. The thin man *was Standartenjunker Josef Richter, whom Sterling had dubbed "Rubberman," due to his ability to stretch and contort his body. The blond man was Obersturmführer Friedrich Mayer, whom Sterling had nicknamed "Fritz," as a play on both the German name used as a slur in the Second World War, as well as on the man's electrical-based powers.*

Fritz shot a bolt of electricity at the squad, but instead of striking his target—the seemingly-vulnerable Luckyman—the bolt arced instead into Dynamo, who simply absorbed the blast. Gargoyle hefted his BAR and immediately opened fire, the rifle roaring as it fired an uninterrupted stream of bullets. Fritz and Rubberman dove in opposite directions. Fritz shot electrical blasts at the group of soldiers, to no effect; those that Dynamo didn't simply absorb either deflected away from Luckyman or impacted harmlessly against the hides of Gargoyle and Mimic. Rubberman stretched like a snake, his body thinning and becoming an even more difficult target.

— § _ —

Dodging another blow, the Shield dropped low to the floor, one leg extended. He spun, sweeping his leg, and caught the Nazi behind the ankles, sending him crashing, off-balance, to the floor. The blond man hit hard, and winced as the back of his head smacked into the floor.

Steel Sterling's information had included intel on this man. He was *Hauptsturmführer* Kurt Wiedler. Two days ago, Wiedler, himself the son of a high-ranking Nazi war criminal, had discovered that he had limited super-strength and invulnerability. He hadn't had time to practice using his powers, however, and had been left in reserve in case of attack on the building. Wiedler was a decent fighter, the Shield noted, but he relied too much on brute strength. He was a thug, through and through, and just went into the fight swinging, giving no thought to tactics or strategy. Wiedler had power, to be sure, but power only took you so far.

The Shield leaped onto Wiedler, pinning him to the floor. He pushed his knee against Wiedler's neck, cutting off both his air supply and the flow of blood to his brain. The Nazi brute thrashed, but the Shield was stronger, and did not relent. Wiedler's face became deeper shades of red by the second. He dug his fingers into the Shield's calf, then his thigh, to no effect.

Wiedler went limp, and his eyes rolled back into their sockets. Lack of blood and oxygen had, at last, taken their toll and caused him to lose consciousness. The Shield lifted himself from Wiedler, and stood. He remained wary, just in case the Nazi showed the uncharacteristic planning needed to play dead, as it were, and wait for the Shield to drop his guard.

The other men had fled the room during the Shield's fight with Wiedler. The Shield looked around, searching for something that he could use to bind the Nazi. Books lay in piles on the floor next to bookshelves that were splintered and demolished during the fight. A table and chairs were smashed. A telephone was strewn across the floor, the Bakelite shell somehow, miraculously, surviving the chaos.

The Shield yanked the telephone cord from the wall, and the end snapped, the connector still in place in the socket. He did the same with the other end, picking up the telephone's base unit, then dropped it with a clang from bell inside as it hit the floor once he had the cord in hand.

Flipping the unconscious Wiedler onto his stomach, the Shield began tying the man's hands and feet together. Given his strength, the Shield wasn't sure how long the cord would last once Wiedler regained consciousness, but it was all he had to work with at the moment.

— § —

Diefenbach screamed as a torrent of flame struck him in the face. He dropped to the pavement, his rifle clattering beside him, forgotten in his agony. The American *übermensch* that could shoot fire from his hands had done just that when Diefenbach had poked his head up to take another shot at the soldiers on the deck of the ship above them.

His face was in agony, but he was not dead. The fighting was still raging around him, and his brothers-in-arms were counting on him to do his part. Squinting through the pain, he retrieved his rifle, then ran out into the open, firing in the direction that Firebrand had been. He kept moving, trying to keep himself from becoming an easier target.

As he dove behind another stack of crates on the opposite side of the pier, his rifle began to make a clicking sound instead of a staccato roar when he pulled the trigger: he was out of ammunition. He looked, desperate, for anything else that he could use as a weapon. A few yards away, he spotted a blowtorch, with a hose connecting it to a small cylinder of gas on a two-wheeled cart. It wouldn't give him much use as a ranged weapon, but a blowtorch still had *possibilities*. He dove for the piece of equipment, and set to work on igniting the flame.

— § —

Fritz jerked as the bullets tore into his body. Ironically, he wasn't even the target: Gargoyle had fired his BAR at Rubberman, but the bullets had bounced off of his tightly-stretched body, and ricocheted into his

Nazi comrade. The blond Nazi collapsed after being struck by nearly a half-dozen high-caliber rounds. Blood soaked through his uniform and began to pool around him on the floor.

"Friedrich!" Rubberman yelled in horror. He stopped twisting and stretching, distracted by what had happened to Fritz. Dynamo took the shot, and struck Rubberman squarely in the chest. The dark-haired Nazi convulsed, and his body snapped back to more normal proportions. He fell to the floor, twitching.

Luckyman pulled out a field telephone from his pack while his teammates began to secure their defeated foes. The radio was large and bulky, contained in a small bag, and had a handset not unlike that of a normal telephone, if smaller.

"Base," he called into the handset, "Luckyman. First floor is secure. Two prisoners, one in need of immediate medical care." A static-laden voice issued through the handset. Luckyman flipped a switch inside the bag, returned the handset to its cradle, zipped the bag, and returned it to his pack. "Medics are on the way," he announced as the rest of the team shoved the insensate Rubberman into a crate, then lashed it down with some rope. "We're clear to proceed once the prisoners are secure." As if on cue, two paramedics, escorted by a half-dozen police officers, burst through the doors to the room.

— § _ —

Rory Weber threw another punch at Steel Sterling, who easily batted the man's hand away.

"Give it up, Rory," Sterling said, stepping aside to evade a strike to his abdomen. "This fight was over before it started."

"You led us into a trap, Johnson," Weber spat. "You're a damned traitor!"

"No, you idiot," Sterling said, grabbing Weber's right wrist as the man attempted another punch. "I'm Steel Sterling. I was *never* on your side, so I can't be a traitor. And that's not the fight I'm talking about."

Weber tried to throw another punch with his left fist, only to have Sterling catch the fist in the palm of his hand with a loud "slap." Weber stared at Sterling in surprise, only for Sterling to regard him with disappointment. He tilted his head back, then slammed his forehead into Weber's. The man slumped in Sterling's grip, unconscious.

The Shield found Dynamo, Gargoyle, Luckyman, and Mimic in the stairwell, headed up. They filled him in on what had happened so far as they climbed to the next floor, and he told them about Wiedler. Luckyman pulled out the field telephone and reported their progress, as well as Wiedler's location for pickup by the authorities downstairs. Soon, they were joined at the third floor by the Black Cobra, who reported that he had secured the third floor and taken out another Nazi agent.

Luckyman relayed the information, then said into the field telephone, "Say again?" He listened, and replied, "Understood." He stowed the field telephone again, then looked up at the Shield, who was in command of Baker Squad. "We've got another player on the board," Luckyman reported. "Before Meteor and Eagle entered the building, someone pushed a shooter from the window on the fourth floor." He glanced at the Black Cobra, then added, "He had an arrow in his chest."

"Good Lord," the Black Cobra breathed. "He swore he only shot to wound."

The Shield nodded. "We'll deal with the Arrow," he said, "if and when we encounter him. In the meantime, the plan still stands. We rendezvous with Meteor and Eagle on the fourth floor and secure the building." Nods of assent came from the squad. "All right. Let's do this." The squad climbed the final flight of stairs, and Luckyman took point.

— § - —

Diefenbach stepped out into the open, his blowtorch at the ready, spewing a gout of flame nearly a foot long. The gas cylinder for the blowtorch was bound in his jacket in a makeshift backpack, the sleeves around his neck and his belt squeezing tightly to contain both his pants and the base of the gas cylinder. He lit a rag, torn from his own clothing, and stuffed into the mouth of a bottle of alcohol he'd found in one of the crates he'd taken shelter behind. He threw the Molotov cocktail, and it shattered near a group of American soldiers. All but one escaped the wave of liquid fire, and his brothers-in-arms rushed to put out the flames consuming his uniform.

Diefenbach ran across the pier, brandishing the torch. He charged some of the American soldiers, who darted out of his path to avoid being immolated as well. Bullets pinged around him, but he charged toward his target undeterred. He raised the blowtorch, ready to do to the American übermensch *what had been done to him, but as he approached, the man simply looked at him and raised a hand, palm out, toward him.*

The flame on the end of the torch simply vanished. Diefenbach could hear the gas continuing to escape, but it refused to reignite. And then he realized what a fool he had been when the man began to speak in his indecipherable English, and Diefenbach was surrounded by soldiers with drawn weapons.

— § —

Gargoyle kicked down the door, and it shattered as it was ripped from its hinges. Inside the enormous room, which took up most of the fourth floor, the squad could see a large, rocket-like device that lay on its side. A seat and handlebars, which looked to have been taken from a motorcycle, were bolted onto the rocket, and small wings sat just below them. In front of the contraption, the Black Knight held an unconscious Meteor by his collar, his arm raised in a fist, mid-strike. Eagle lay nearby, also incapacitated.

As the squad quickly filed into the room, everyone brought their weapons to bear on the Black Knight. He looked briefly at the six heavily-armed men pointing weapons in his direction, and dropped Meteor limply to the floor. He turned and ran for the rocket as bullets and bolts of electricity shot around him. Bullets pinged, ricocheting off of his armor and the skin of the rocket as he leaped onto the seat.

An enormous trapdoor dropped open in the ceiling, and with the flick of a button, the rocket roared to life. The platform that the rocket sat upon tilted suddenly, and the rocket shot out through the opening in the ceiling, and into the night sky. With the squad's fliers incapacitated, there was no way to follow him. Once again, the Black Knight had escaped.

Chapter Twenty-One
Monday, April 4, 1954

Three weeks had passed since the attack by and defeat of Donner's forces. Nearly all of the Nazis and their allies had been arrested, and were facing lengthy prison terms once their trials were over. Some, like Helmut Schulz, were being remanded to the World Court to answer for war crimes committed during the Second World War. A handful had managed to escape, and a manhunt was underway, but with little success.

Three of the Nazis from the attack had been placed under armed guard while their wounds were treated: Günter Diefenbach, whose face had suffered severe burns, Ulrich Schmidt, whose jaw had been pulverized by a round from Samson's BAR, and Sigmund Ritter, who had been found after the Black Knight's escape, a swastika carved across his face and a bloodied arrow laying near him on the floor. The Arrow had not been seen in the weeks since the battle, and both the police and the other heroes were looking for him, as well.

Schmidt, Diefenbach, and Ritter lay in their hospital beds, together in a single room. Two police officers stood watch outside the door. Schmidt remained heavily sedated; he had undergone several surgeries to repair his destroyed face, and more were likely in the future. A metal appliance had been attached in an experimental surgery, replacing the demolished bone with a new jaw of dark metal. The doctors planned to implement an equally experimental skin graft procedure, to cover the metal with skin taken from a cadaver, but for the moment, Schmidt's chin was an exposed piece of metal. His cheeks hung loosely, almost like a bulldog's, and his artificial lower teeth were exposed with no lip to cover them.

Diefenbach and Ritter were both conscious, and their wounds were well on their way to healing, but they would both be left with hideous scars. They spoke to one another in quiet German, and a soft tapping interrupted their conversation. A head poked into view through the window. Diefenbach and Ritter were shocked, since they were on the hospital's sixth floor, and window washers would not be working this late at night. The head moved further into view, and one hand clung to the smooth surface of the window: it was Georg Schreiber, whom the American *übermensch* recruits had called the Creeper. He tapped on the window pane with a finger once again, then put his finger to his lips.

Diefenbach stood and quietly opened the window. Schreiber crawled in, and dragged a large bag in behind him. He set it down gently on the floor as Diefenbach closed the window once again. Quickly unzipping the bag, Schreiber began pulling out firearms. He handed a rifle to Diefenbach, then another to Ritter. He then passed out bags filled with magazines of ammunition to the other men. He pulled out an odd-looking harness assembly, then stepped over to Schmidt's bedside.

Catching on after a moment, Diefenbach and Ritter joined Schreiber at Schmidt's bedside, where Schreiber was disconnecting the IV from the unconscious man's arm. They helped him lift Schmidt's upper body, and Schreiber passed the harness under him, then attached it around Schmidt's chest. They lifted Schmidt into a seated position, and Schreiber secured the rest of the harness around his own chest. He stood, and Schmidt's limp body hung suspended from his back.

"Make your way to the roof," Schreiber whispered in German. He stepped to the window and continued, "I will meet you there." He opened the window, crawled out, and began to crawl up the side of the building.

Diefenbach and Ritter inserted magazines into their rifles as quietly as they could. They exchanged a glance, nodding at one another, then racked the slides on their rifles with a loud "click-clack" as the bolts chambered a round, readying the rifles for use.

"What was that?" a muffled man's voice said in English on the other side of the door.

"Sounded like," another man's voice began, but trailed off.

"Couldn't be," the first voice said. Shadows of the two police officers filled the frosted glass of the door's window. The doorknob began to turn, and Diefenbach and Ritter opened fire. They moved quickly into the hallway, and stepped over the bullet-riddled bodies of the two police officers, whose blood was forming a thick, sticky, red puddle in sharp contrast to the antiseptic white linoleum tile of the hospital floor. A woman in a white nurse's uniform screamed for a moment before they opened fire once again, killing her instantly, just as they had the police officers guarding their room. They made their way swiftly up the stairs, and it was a relatively short trip to the roof. They only needed to kill a few other people who got in their way.

When they reached the roof, they found what looked like a helicopter waiting for them, except where there should have been rotor blades, wings were mounted atop the craft that rotated in the middle, and the jet engines mounted on the outer halves of the wings were pointed down at the rooftop. Schreiber was inside the open cabin where the wings met the fuselage, securing Schmidt into a seat in the back. The Black Knight sat at the controls, watching them, and waiting for everyone to get strapped in before the vehicle lifted off from the roof. Once in the air, the wings rotated, and the unusual aircraft shot off into the night.

— §. —

Alex Stevens set down the newspaper on the kitchen table. A weight he hadn't even realized he'd been carrying seemed to be lifting from his shoulders. Senator McCarthy's influence had slowly been waning in the last few months, and in a last-ditch effort to regain support, he had accused the Army—the *Army!*—of being "soft on communists."

This time, the hearings he was heading on the House Un-American Activities Commission were being televised, and the public was finally seeing McCarthy for the bully that he was. He was losing public support in droves, which meant that the threat of HUAC coming after superheroes was becoming more and more remote.

He set the paper down and made his way to the roof. It was a beautiful day out, and he wanted to take in the spring air. The air this morning was crisp, and the sun was shining. There were only a few fluffy, white clouds in the deep blue sky. He closed his eyes, and took a deep breath. He held it for a moment, then let it out, smiling.

"Beautiful," he said.

"Aw, shucks," a voice said playfully from behind him. "Thanks for saying so, mister." Stevens' eyes shot open and he spun around. A young woman was standing on the roof behind him. She *was* beautiful, he noticed. She also looked familiar somehow, and his eyes narrowed, then widened in surprise.

"Marjorie?" Stevens asked, dumbfounded. "Marjorie Breslin?"

"That's me," she replied with a laugh. "I know it's been a few years since you saw me last, but I didn't think you'd have *that* much trouble recognizing me, Alex."

"You're," he began, at a loss for words. "You've... *grown.*" He mentally kicked himself, and she laughed again.

"People do that," she said. The last time Stevens had seen Marjorie, she had barely been fifteen years old. She was one of his sister's friends, and he had barely paid attention to "the kid," as he'd often called her. She, on the other hand, had been smitten with him since the first time they'd met. Now, Stevens was having a hard time keeping his eyes off of her. "I heard about you and Evelyn," she said after a moment. "I'm... I'm sorry that things didn't work out."

"Me too," Stevens agreed.

"I hope I don't sound too forward or something," Marjorie said, "but you weren't a good match. You... you could do a lot better." She looked pointedly at him. The crush, it seemed, had never gone away.

"I," Stevens began, but he stopped himself. He had no idea what to say.

"It was because you're Nucleus," Marjorie blurted out. "Wasn't it?"

"Wha—?" Stevens sputtered, shock and confusion leaving him dumbfounded once again. Then anger rose up in him, and he began, "Did Megan—"

"No," Marjorie interrupted. "It wasn't hard to figure out, Alex." His surprise returned, and Marjorie caught it in his expression. "But *she* never did, did she?" She scoffed. "That girl is so self-centered."

"How?" Stevens managed to ask, at last.

"Even with the mask," she said, "you're still *you*. Megan told me about your friend when you first came home. When he said he was Strongman a couple months later, it was pretty obvious." After a moment, she added. "I will never tell, Alex. I care about you. I always have. Even if this doesn't go the way I want it to, I would never do that to you." Stevens stepped forward, closing the gap between them. He smiled.

"Lunch?" he asked. Marjorie laughed once more.

— § —

"There's a place for superheroes in New York, Mr. Mayor," Percy van Norton said. "We just have to iron out exactly what that is, and what the rules will be, going forward."

Van Norton sat across from the mayor at a large, rectangular oak table in one of the many formal meeting rooms in the van Norton estate. Van Norton wore a well-pressed, dark gray suit, and was flanked by a pair of equally well-appointed lawyers on either side. Across the table, Mayor Richard Wagner was similarly dressed in a black suit, and had his own contingent of lawyers flanking him at the table.

Van Norton tapped the stack of papers in front of him on the table. "I trust that you've had a chance to review the documents my team sent to your office?"

The mayor hefted an identical stack of papers that sat in front of him. "Indeed I have, Mr. van Norton," Mayor Wagner replied. "I must say, it's a very... *inventive* solution to the issues before us."

"Having people running around unchecked," van Norton said, "like in a comic book or the wild west is an untenable solution, Mr. Mayor. Society needs boundaries, or everything descends into chaos."

"I agree with your sentiment," Mayor Wagner replied, "but getting even half of this through the city council is a daunting proposition, to say nothing of the inevitable battles at the state and federal levels."

"One fight at a time," van Norton said. He indicated the lawyers at his sides. "My people are working on that angle, as well."

"You have my support," Mayor Wagner said. "I look forward to working with you."

— § —

John "Steel" Sterling leaned over the railing on the edge of the deck of his yacht. The surf crashed against the prow of the ship, spraying him with a cool mist of salt water. Dora Cummings approached him from behind, and wrapped her arms around him as she leaned her head against his shoulder. He relaxed, the tension in his muscles ebbing away at her touch.

"Good morning," he said to her, turning so that their faces met.

"Good morning," she replied. They kissed softly, then turned to watch the early rays of dawn peeking over the horizon. They had been aboard the yacht for two weeks, and were now halfway to their destination in South America. Officially, they were taking a vacation and going on a cruise aboard Sterling's yacht, which he'd inherited from his father, with Dora's father and their friend, Officer Clancy. Unofficially, they were on a mission to track down other Nazi cells affiliated with Donner, and take them out. They had battled the Black Knight, operating under the alias Dr. Yar, on a previous journey to Brazil, and given the Black Knight's ties to Donner, as well as Donner's own history in Argentina, that couldn't be a coincidence. That alone warranted another trip, as far as Sterling was concerned.

Sterling and Dora had started seeing one another shortly after their first trip to South America, to rescue her father, the industrialist and accomplished scientist Dr. Walter Cummings, from the Black Knight. In the months since, they had only grown closer. To Sterling's relief, not only did her father approve, he had become a friend of Sterling's in his own right.

The two watched the sun climb over the horizon. This far into their voyage, there was nothing but water as far as the eye could see, and the water reflected the rainbow of brilliant colors from the sunrise like a mirror stretched across the horizon. They held one another in their arms in silence, taking in the sounds of the waves and the ocean breeze.

— § —

The mugger ran down the alley, firing his pistol indiscriminately into the dark shadows behind him. Every few seconds, a glimpse of something dark became visible, moving through the shadows of the poorly-lit alleyway, before vanishing into the darkness once more.

The thug was so focused on the dark figure pursuing him, he never saw what was in front of him. He barreled, face first, into another black-clad brick wall of a man. The impact caused the mugger to bounce back in the direction he'd come. He fell to the ground, landing on his rear end, and the pistol clattered away into the alley behind him. He stared up at the Black Cobra in horror.

"Aw, cripes," he muttered in shock. "There's *two* a yas? Two Black Cobras?" The second black-clad figure stepped out of the shadows, kicking the pistol further out of the thug's reach as he approached. He was smaller than the Black Cobra, but no less well-muscled, and he wore an identical costume.

"Hey," he said, mock irritation in his voice. "*He's* the Black Cobra. *I'm* the Cobra Kid!" He smacked his fist into the palm of his other hand, and cracked his knuckles. The thug glanced between the two men in identical costumes, and gulped loudly.

AFTERWARD

This novel is populated by a large cast of characters drawn from the public domain, and would not have been possible without the contributions of their creators. Many thanks to the Public Domain Super Heroes wiki (http://pdsh.wikia.com) and the Digital Comics Museum (https://digitalcomicmuseum.com). The information provided on those sites was invaluable in the creation of this novel.

Erich Eidelmann/Donner is based upon the character Volkssturm created by Brandon Longstreth and released as an open source character.

Percy van Norton/Strongman is based upon the character published by the Holyoke Publishing Company.

Don Wright/Captain Freedom and the ***New York Daily Bulletin*** are based upon the characters and settings created by Arthur Cazeneuve & "Franklin Flagg" and published by Harvey Comics.

Chuck Hardy/Samson is based upon the character Chuck Hardy created by Frank Thomas and published by Centaur.

Jack Knapp/Blue Flame is an amalgamation of the characters Jack Richard Knapp/Blue Fire created by Lew Glanzman and published by Centaur, and Blue Flame published by Four Star.

Lewis Binder/Silver Streak is based upon the character Silver Streak, created by Jack Binder and published by Lev Gleason.

Fred Larkin/Lightning is based upon the character created by Bob Powell and published by Fiction House.

Joe Higgins/The Shield is based upon the character created by Harry Shorten & Irv Norvick and published by MLJ Comics.

Ray O'Reilly/Firebrand is an amalgamation of the characters Ray O'Light/Firebrand created by Charles Sultan and published by Harry A. Chesler/Harvey Comics, and Rod Reilly/Firebrand created by S.M. Iger and Reed Crandall and published by Quality.

Jaspar Crow is based upon the character created by Lou Fine and published by Quality Comics.

Schmachenberg is based upon the character Schmachenberg/Cerebex, created by Bill Benulis and published by Fiction House.

Chen Chang is based upon the character created by Munson Paddock and published by Fox Feature Syndicate.

John "Steel" Sterling, Dora Cummings, Dr. Walter Cummings, Officer Clancy and related characters are based upon the characters created by Abner Sundell and Charles Biro and published by MLJ.

Dr. Conrad Krueger/the Black Knight is an amalgam of the character the Black Knight created by Abner Sundell and Charles Biro and published by MLJ, and the character Dr. Conrad Krueger/the Black Knight created by Mike Sekowsky and published by Sterling.

Jim Hornsby/the Black Cobra, Bob Hornsby/the Cobra Kid, D.A. Hornsby and related characters are based upon the characters published by Harry A. Chesler/Four Star.

The Arrow is based upon the character Ralph Payne/the Arrow created by Paul Gustavson and published by Centaur.

Johann "John" Weber/Count Berlin is based upon the character Count Berlin created by John Cassone and published by MLJ.

The Boss is based upon the character created by Jack Binder and published by Fawcett Comics.

Georg Schreiber/the Creeper is based upon the character the Creeper created by Joe Blair and Irv Norvick and published by MLJ.

Ulrich Schmidt/Iron Jaw is based upon the character von Schmidt/Iron Jaw created by Charles Biro and published by Lev Gleason.

Jim Andrews/Dynamo is based upon the character created by Robert Webb (as "Harold Weber") and published by Fox Features Syndicate.

Duke O'Dowd/Meteor is based upon the character Duke O'Dowd/the Human Meteor published by Harvey Comics.

Danny Barr/Luckyman is based upon the character published by Cambridge House.

Brett Hannigan is based upon the character created by Lou Cameron and published by Ace.

Xavier Exeley/Black Fist is based upon the character created by Vito Delsante, an open source character based upon the public domain character Black Hand created by Joe Blair and Lin Streeter and published by MLJ.

Julius Iles/the Eel is based upon the character Professor Aqua/Eel published by Ace.

Helmut Schulz is based upon the character Captain Murder created by John Cassone and published by MLJ.

Günter Diefenbach is based upon the character Firebug created by Bill Fraccio and published by Hillman.

Josef Richter/Rubberman is based upon the character Herr Riktor/Rubberman created by Harry Sussman and published by Hillman.

Friedrich Mayer/Fritz is based upon the character Fritz created by Al Bryant and published by Harvey Comics.

Kurt Wiedler is based upon the character Kurt Wiedler/Son of the Hun published by MLJ.

Sigmund Ritter is based upon the character Captain Swastika published by MLJ.

About the Author

Jeffrey Harlan is an independent author of superhero fiction and the founder of Confluent Press, an independent publishing imprint that provides editorial and design services to self-published and independent authors.

In 2012, he began publishing *The Protectorate*, an independent comic book series about a team of teenaged superheroes in Las Vegas, before realizing that not only was drawing an ongoing comic book much more difficult than he'd expected, he also enjoyed writing the stories far more than he did drawing them. In 2021, inspired by other prose superhero novels he'd read, he self-published *Donner und Blitzkrieg*, a prequel to *The Protectorate* that focused on that world's first superheroes. He soon followed that up with three novellas, adapted from the four completed issues of *The Protectorate*. The novellas greatly expanded on the original comics and completed the storyline from the incomplete and unpublished fifth issue. In 2022, Jeffrey edited the novellas into a single volume, which he published as *Invasion*.

A military brat, Jeffrey moved frequently throughout his life. He's been a journalist, an airman, an educator, a security officer, and more. He's lived in three countries and seven states, and has traveled the world. A lifelong Trekkie, he has a deep love of science fiction and superheroes. He lives in Southern California's San Bernardino Mountains with his wife, Megan, their dog, Lucky, and their cats, Dusty and Snowball.